REVENGE

REVENGE

A Grayson Cooper Adventure

Outer Banks Series – Episode 2

by Douglas Brisotti

ISBN: 9798633386462
Printed in the USA

Any references to historical events, real people, or real places are used fictitiously. Names, characters, and places are products of the author's imagination.

First printing edition 2020.

Published by:
Next Chapter Holdings, LLC
3741 Greene's Crossing
Greensboro, NC 27410

For my parents.

Patricia Brisotti (deceased)
Lee Lang Brisotti
Richard Brisotti, Sr.

You made me who I am.

North Carolina's Outer Banks

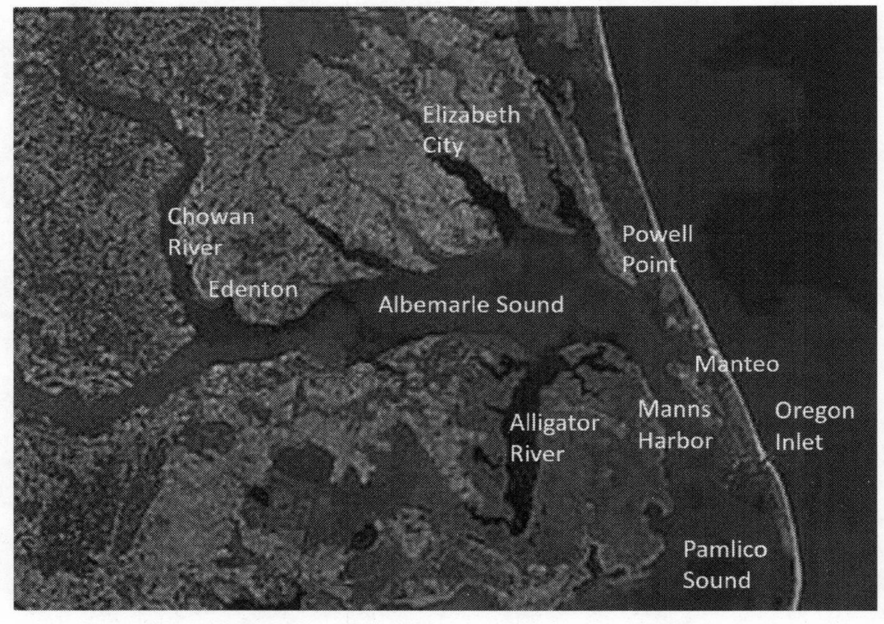

Table of Contents

Common Boating Terms

Bow – the front of the boat

Stern – the rear of the boat

Port – the left side of the boat

Starboard – the right side of the boat

Forward – moving towards the front end of the boat

Aft – moving towards the rear end of the boat

Underway – when the boat is moving

Ahead – when the boat is moving in a forward direction

Astern – when the boat is moving in a backwards direction

Bulkhead – a wall in a boat

Topside – moving to the upper deck of the boat

Below – moving to the below deck or cabin of the boat

Salon – the main living area on a boat; the living room

Galley – the kitchen on a boat

Head – the bathroom on a boat

Chapter 1

Oscar is pissed. He's sitting at the wheel of his black Mercedes driving through a pelting rain, trying to keep his emotions in check. He breathes deeply in, filling his lungs with air, holding it for four seconds before exhaling slowly. He repeats this slow breathing four more times until he feels some of the stress leave his body. The rain bombards the windshield making it difficult to see. He turns the wipers up to the fastest speed, each working from the center, pulling the water up and out to the sides keeping his view mostly clear.

His mind is anything *but* clear, however. He is in a rage. Years of preparation setting up his system, tens of thousands in capital used to purchase a boat and to encourage certain authorities to look the other way, and all the personal energy he has expended training staff and keeping the operation running, all gone in one night. And with it, the millions of dollars of income he makes in the process.

He looks down to check his speed; he is twenty over the limit, angrily pushing down on the accelerator with his right foot. For a moment he presses harder envisioning his boot crushing the head of whomever is responsible for upending tonight's events. He then thinks better of it and lifts his foot slowing the sedan to just five over the speed limit. The last thing he needs now is to be pulled over by the police.

Unfortunately, Oscar knows little right now. One of his men was there to meet the boat when the events happened, and he described to Oscar what transpired at the dock. Calling it a dock is a bit of a reach; it is a railroad tie suspended in pine brush along the shore where the sportfish pulls in long enough to disembark passengers entering the United States illegally through the wetlands of North Carolina. From the *dock*, they are then ushered through shallow water over a submerged deck to vehicles waiting nearby to move them inland.

The man saw the sportfish pulling up to the dock and noticed another vessel behind it, running fast in their direction. The other boat looked like a police boat, but it didn't have any flashing lights. No doubt though, it was coming to intercept them on the shoreline. One of Oscar's men standing in the cockpit of the fishing boat was initially able to turn the vessel away by firing on it with his AK 47. The other boat turned away to protect itself, but only for a moment. The storm was approaching from the sea and suddenly out of the rain there were more boats following the first one. These were obviously police boats, their lights flashing blue across the small ripples of the river, each vessel carrying more men and more firepower. Oscar's team was no match for the superior police forces, and they were quickly overwhelmed.

Oscar was specifically focused on the first vessel and asked the man more questions about it. He told Oscar it was a center console with a name on the side that he believed to be *Recovery,* although he couldn't be sure. He only captured glimpses of it when lightening would brighten the dark, rainy night. It was the one that he didn't think was a police boat, but it *was* the first boat to engage Oscar's team. In the lightening he also saw two people on the boat, a man and a woman, the man running the boat, the woman firing on the sportfish with a handgun. While she was good with the weapon, her pistol was no match for the AKs that returned fire from the shore, and so it was forced to turn back. It wasn't long, though, before reinforcements arrived and they returned to the fight.

He described to Oscar seeing the man get shot and go down, the vessel slowing before stopping completely in the water. When the fighting was over, the man on the first boat was given assistance by the police and what looked like paramedics on board, moved to one of the other boats and whisked quickly away by water. The man knew the fight was over, and so he ran to tell Oscar what he witnessed.

Oscar assumed the police boat was taking the man to the closest emergency room, Chowan Hospital in the town of Edenton. This is Oscar's destination.

The police boat Captain is running full throttle in the rain heading south on the Chowan River. Time is of the essence for his passenger who was shot in the neck during the raid on the smuggling boat. Medics aboard his vessel are fighting to stop the bleeding as best they can, trying to stabilize him before transfer to the waiting ambulance at The 51 House Restaurant in Edenton.

Flashing blue lights make sure that they are highly visible to other vessels that might be out, although in this weather it is unlikely there will be any. Brand-new electronics give the captain visibility that isn't obtainable with the naked eye in the stormy conditions. They speed under Highway 17 entering Albemarle Sound, and immediately turn to port heading for the eastern shoreline running parallel on the south side of the Edenhouse Bridge.

On shore the red lights of a waiting ambulance flash through the rain and the captain steers directly at it, slowing only moments before entering the small marina next to the restaurant. He steers the vessel to port approaching the north side of the marina at a forty-five-degree angle to shore. He puts the engines in neutral allowing the momentum to carry the vessel farther in, and then turns the wheel all the way to starboard, bringing the port side parallel to the dock. A moment before the bow strikes the wood structure, he puts the engines into reverse and spins the wheel all the way over to port, stopping the vessel completely, resting it gently against the seawall.

Paramedics are already standing on the dock and the crew on the boat wastes no time transferring the man to the waiting gurney. Quickly they roll him across the grass and into the waiting ambulance. The doors are barely shut before it speeds off under US 17 toward the Hospital, a short five-minute drive for the speeding ambulance.

Oscar arrives at the emergency room, parks at the far south side of the parking lot and sits for a moment to calm himself. He checks his ankle to be sure his revolver is still there, a nervous habit that is comforting, but unnecessary. Not once has the gun not been there. He looks at himself in the rear-view mirror.

His dark hair is slicked back, partially because of the rain, partially because he likes it that way. He messes it up a little bit in order to look more like a frantic family member of a patient in the small-town emergency room. Much of the population around the area is Hispanic, as Oscar is, but many do honest work as day laborers or as a crewmember in a construction trade. Oscar's flashy Mercedes, pressed black jeans and expensive cowboy boots will surely make him stand out, and so he does what he can to blend in. He is glad, too, that his beard is full and covering much of the detail of his face.

He enters through the automatic sliding doors and immediately turns to the right, away from the main desk and toward what looks like a waiting area. Families are gathered together, faces creased with worry. Oscar makes his way to a corner where he can easily observe all that is happening in the small emergency room. He doesn't have to wait long.

After only fifteen minutes an Edenton Police cruiser screeches to a stop in front of the sliding doors and a woman jumps out. She is soaking wet and there is obvious concern on her face. She goes directly to the admitting window.

"Grayson Cooper. Where is he please?" she more demands than asks.

"I'm sorry ma'am, I can't give you..."

The woman pulls something from her pocket and slams it against the glass in front of the woman. It is a badge. "I am Sheriff's Deputy Zaina Majik, I need to know where the patient is right now!"

The woman at the counter looks like she doesn't know what to do. Just then, an Edenton Police officer runs in behind the Sheriff's Deputy. "Paula, we need to see Grayson Cooper right now!"

"Trauma two, Jeb," Paula answers, pressing a button on the desk next to her. The magnetically locked doors whisk open allowing them access, and they run through and vanish into the brightly lit hallway.

Oscar feigns looking for cigarettes on his body being sure to keep his face pointed away from any surveillance cameras. He shakes his head and gets up walking in the direction of the front doors. Before he can reach them an ambulance screeches to a halt in front of the entrance. A gurney is taken from the back and quickly rolled past him heading around the check-in desk down the hallway the officers had just disappeared into.

Oscar shows no recognition on his face when he sees the familiar man being brought in, blood covering much of the gurney. He pauses only a moment before strolling out the front doors, into the rain and back to his Mercedes.

Chapter 2

Fiberglass resin dust fills the air around me, my goggles and breathing mask keeping the harsh particles out of my eyes and mouth. I am sanding one of the many holes in my Whaler. I am no expert at this, which is obvious when you see the rest of my outfit; shorts, a t-shirt and flip flops are not fiberglass working attire. I stop sanding and reach for my coffee. A white film floats on top of the dark liquid, and I remind myself to next time use a travel mug. I pour the coffee out onto the ground.

Investigating my work, I lean in close to the dusty finish, the sun behind me projecting the outline of my head and shoulders onto the side of the hull. I study my shadow as I lean my head to the left stretching the muscle and skin on the right side of my neck. The doctors have told me that I should try to touch left ear to my left shoulder. The first time I do this each day I see bright white sparkles in my eyes as the scar tissue breaks down, the sensation that accompanies it like needles attached to a golf ball being rolled over my skin. Involuntarily I reach up with my right hand and finger the scar on the side of my neck where doctors have done the repair work.

Three weeks ago, I was involved in a gun battle that ended for me when I took a bullet through the meaty part on the right side of my neck. No, I am not a cop, nor was I the bad guy; at least not this time I wasn't. I was working with the police department and Sheriff's office pursuing what turned out to be a human smuggling boat.

I look at my boat and the holes it has that were caused in the same incident. They are mostly fixed now as well. "Good girl, *Recovery*," I tell her, running my finger across the latest repair, soothing her and checking my work at the same time. *We will both have permanent scars*, I think to myself. Not my first ones, that's for sure.

"I am Grayson Cooper, and I am an alcoholic," I say to the group sitting in a circle at the Dare County Center just a mile from Shallowbag Bay Marina in Manteo where I live on my 43' Hatteras.

"Hi, Coop," they say back to me in unison. I am not new here, so they know my nickname even better than they know the one given to me at birth.

I was born here in Manteo and grew up on the northern shore of Roanoke Island. I left after high school to use my Communications Arts degree from East Carolina University in the advertising business in New York City. I retired just before my fortieth birthday and returned here. Calling it *retirement* isn't exactly correct. I had worked hard and made good money, yes, but I also required a significant amount of alcohol in order to produce the way I did, and it almost killed me… three times. Let's just say that my employer and I agreed that they would financially assist me in my transition out of the business and I wouldn't sue them for benefitting from my sickness. They ignored my problem and profited greatly in the process.

I finger the scar again as I tell the group about my most recent struggles brought on by the management of the pain I have been in since being shot. They are all familiar with my story. The human smuggling ring that I was part of disrupting was all over the news; it is one of the biggest stories of the year in this area. My name was not in the reporting because the Sheriff's office had concerns for my safety and never released it to the press. The kingpin of the smuggling operation was not on-site during the take-down, and leads are scarce. Those apprehended that night spoke of "Jefe," but not one seemed to know his real name.

Their concerns increased when I was shown a picture of the smuggling boat Captain and realized that I had possibly seen him with two other men at lunch one afternoon at my buddy Duke's diner, a place called, you guessed it, *Duke's Diner*. One of the men was obviously in charge and is now a person of interest in the case. The only description is from me; a tall guy with a beard and mustache, speaking Spanish and wearing a black cowboy hat, bolo tie and cowboy boots. I didn't pay much attention so it's not much of a description, but it's all the police have to go on right now.

I was involved in the operation, but it was Dare County Sheriff's Deputy Zaina Majik who ran the show and is the reason I was there in the first place. I run my Boston Whaler Guardian, *Recovery*, as a marine patrol contractor for the Dare County Sheriff. Our shores here in North Carolina's Outer Banks claim the lives of so many unsuspecting tourists that it is more economical to outsource the recovery of those bodies to me than to use Sheriff's Office resources. A body that we recovered in early summer, however, had a bullet hole in the center of the forehead.

The victim was a young, Mexican man, and there were no leads or matching missing person reports. Local authorities seemed to be willing to just let it go, but Deputy Majik couldn't do that. She was reminded too much of her brother who disappeared in his junior year of high school, and then was found dead behind an ABC store in Raleigh a few short months later.

Arjun had his problems, no question about that. Arrests for drugs and theft became common before his disappearance, and the discovery of his dead body seemed to be the end to his story, at least for authorities. No one cared about another dead brown boy who lived on the fringes, and so his death was never properly investigated.

I gave Deputy Majik the nickname Magic, a play on her last name, and an apt description for her if I do say so myself. Most people use it now and she likes it. That makes me happy. I should mention that Magic is also my girlfriend. *Girlfriend.* It seems to be such an archaic term, especially at my age. I still like saying it, though.

"Magic is my girlfriend."

The group, already quiet, seems to quiet even more. Each is looking intently at me, some smirking a little. I guess I said it out loud. I seem to have a problem with this, thoughts shaping into words that somehow tumble from my mouth. I smile awkwardly at them, seeing judgement in their eyes. They think she is too young; they think she is too good for me. They are correct about both.

"Does that make you feel better about yourself, Coop?" a woman says with a smile.

"No crosstalk, Sharon," I say using the rules of this meeting to avoid answering. I am smiling too though. We all know Magic is the best part of me.

"How are you feeling?" Sharon asks after the meeting is over and we are socializing over orange juice and coffee.

"Good," I say. "One day at a time."

"I mean the gunshot wound, Coop," Sharon clarifies. I knew what she meant.

"Oh, that! I forgot completely about that," I say, again avoiding an answer.

"Well, we were all thinking about you. We said a prayer for your quick healing, both physically and mentally."

"Physically, I'm good," I finally answer. "Mentally, it's going to take a lot more than prayer to solve my mental problems." If I could, I would pat myself on the back for that skillful evasion.

Sharon rests her hand on my forearm and says, "I'll pray for you."

This is where I get a bit uncomfortable. I know I should probably say, *I'll pray for you too*, but that is out of character for me, and so I simply nod. Sharon smiles and walks away.

I walk over to the window and look out at traffic. It's a fairly slow day in Manteo and only a single black Mercedes is pulling out of the parking lot turning north into light traffic on Highway 64.

Chapter 3

"Two eggs over easy, bacon, grits and a cup of coffee. And make it quick young man," I say.

"I'll show you quick, Coop," Duke replies in his deep, gravelly voice, showing me the back of his hand. He is an intimidating figure, just under six feet tall, almost three hundred pounds, more of it muscle than fat. He is completely bald now, although he used to shave his head when we were younger so that it would fit into his football helmet. Recent treatments for cancer took his hair and it never grew back, even now that he is in remission. Duke has been my friend for over thirty years, and I am a regular at his aforementioned establishment, *Duke's Diner,* located just across the Dare Memorial Bridge in Mann's Harbor. I have been coming here since his dad, also named Duke, ran the place. Duke II left school during his junior year at Catawba College when his dad got sick. His father died a few short years later and my friend has been here ever since.

"Yeah, yeah. Just don't screw up my order Gar-cone," I say, ribbing him like I did when we were younger.

"You do know who is preparing your food, don't you Poop?" he replies, using the nickname he knows I hate.

"I figure you can't do any worse than your seventy-nine health rating, Number Two," I counter using the nickname he equally dislikes.

"That's ninety-seven."

"Oh, I'm dyslexic."

"You're a jackass."

"No arguments there," a woman's voice chimes in from Duke's left.

Duke looks toward the door and sees Magic coming toward us. She is in her Dare County Sheriff's Department uniform, a tan Performance Gear long-sleeve shirt, army green shorts and military style boots with socks that reach just to the top of each boot. Her dark skin accentuates the muscles in her thighs and calves. I like it.

"What do you see in this guy, Magic?" Duke asks.

"I ask myself that every day, Duke," Magic replies as she removes her Dare County hat allowing her dark hair to tumble down her back.

"I'm sitting right here," I say.

"Coop, in all of your life has anyone *ever* not known you were in a room?" Duke asks, apparently referring to my inability to be quiet for any noticeable period of time.

"I have no response to that," I reply as Magic slides in next to me. They both look at me, astonishment on their faces. "Whatever," I say using three fingers of my right hand upward, and then turning them so they face my left shoulder, forming the "W" and then the "E" as I say it.

"I'll just have a cup of coffee Duke," Magic says, shaking her head at my response. Duke rolls his eyes at me and then nods at Magic, turning and walking toward the coffee pot on the other side of the counter.

"You are covered in dust, Coop," Magic says. "You didn't go to your meeting like that, did you?" she asks.

"No crosstalk!" I say trying to use meeting rules to halt any more ridicule.

"As much as you would like that to be true, it's not," she says, smiling at me. She picks up my napkin, dips it in my water and proceeds to wipe a clean spot on my left cheek. She then kisses my face in that now clean spot. "How are you doing today?" she asks more seriously.

"I'm good," I say, taking the napkin in my hand and wiping my lips, a conspiratorial grin growing on my face.

"If you try it, I will have to take you down and cuff you."

"That's just more incentive, you know that, right?" I say with a smile. I know we can't be too public with displays of affection, especially when she is working.

"Seriously, Coop, how was everything today?" Magic knows I am being evasive.

"Good. Keeping busy fixing *Recovery* has helped, and then talking with the group props me up." I say. "What's the latest on our case?"

"*Our* case?" Magic questions back. "Did you ask Vanna to remove a vowel from Coop so you can pretend that you are now a Cop?" I truly have no response for this one. She continues, "There is actual training that we go through to earn this uniform," placing her thumb behind the embroidered emblem of the Dare County Sheriff that is on her left breast pocket and lifting it toward me.

"Can I do that?" I ask, reaching for her pocket.

Magic smacks my hand away, laughing and leaning her head into my left shoulder. "You are an adolescent boy, you know that?" she continues, lifting her head and looking up into my eyes. Every time she does this it startles me how my body reacts. Physically, I can feel it in my skin. She communicates how she feels about me with a simple glance and I internally hope that I can be the person she thinks I am.

"I never said I wasn't," I say, quoting a favorite fictional character of mine.

"You need to stop reading *Dan Coast* Mysteries," she says.

I look at her, a look of astonishment on my face. "Never!" I say. She laughs. She also knows I am telling the truth. I haven't missed a Dan Coast book yet, and I never will. "So, what brings you here?" I ask. Then, raising my voice a little so Duke can hear me, "It definitely isn't the food!"

"Screw you, Coop," comes the deep reply from the kitchen. There is nothing like the banter between old friends.

"Well," she pauses a moment. "I wanted to bring you up to date on the case."

"Our case," I correct her. She leans her chin down and looks at me by raising her eyes to the top of their sockets. I know this look. It's the, *don't push it, Coop* look. I smile back innocently.

"We still don't have any leads on who *Jefe* is," she says, referring to the kingpin of the smuggling operation. "We went through the buildings on the land near Edenton but there was almost nothing there. We pulled fingerprints off a table, a few chairs and a fan. We were only able to match one set and those were Miguel's," she says.

Magic is referring to Miguel Cortez, the Captain of the sportfish that we intercepted that night. At the end of the gunfight, Magic encountered Miguel sitting at the flybridge helm of the vessel, a gunshot wound under his ribcage causing his life to slowly drain from his body. Miguel was an unwilling participant in the operation, indentured into service through the kidnapping of his daughter, Angela. As he felt his life slipping away, Miguel handed Magic a photo of his little Angel. In a weak voice he implored her to please find his daughter. She whispered into the man's ear, "Lo prometo." I promise.

"Any leads on his daughter?" I ask.

"No," she says, sadness in both her eyes and her voice. Magic doesn't like not keeping her promises.

"So, what is the prognosis here?" I ask.

"Wow, an SAT word. Very good Coop."

"Thank you," I say with a smile like a schoolkid pleased with his teacher's praise.

"There is almost nothing to go on. We are tracing the path back and so far we have gotten to Jacksonville, Florida," she says. "We'll get them. Either we will get a break in our investigation, or they will make a mistake."

"We'll get them," I say. Magic gives me that look again. "I mean, *you'll* get them," I add, emphasizing my words with an eye roll and hand gestures.

"You are such a child," she smiles.

"I never said I wasn't."

Chapter 4

Oscar turns left out of the Dare County Center onto Highway 64 heading north toward downtown Manteo. He passes the Dollar General on his left and moves into the right lane. A block later he makes a right between Darrell's Seafood Restaurant and McDonald's onto North Bay Club Drive. There are stone walls and neatly clipped bushes on each side of the narrow entrance driveway to Shallowbag Bay Club & Marina.

As he comes out of the chute-like entrance he keeps to the right of the *Striper's* Bar & Grill sign continuing onto South Bay

Club Drive. To his right, barely ten feet off the roadway, four-story condo buildings rise straight up into the sky, car port at ground level supporting three living floors above. On his left, cars are parked straight into a curb that connects to a sidewalk. Behind that is a wooden, three-rail fence guarding white stone ground cover that bleeds down to the dock at the top of the seawall. Boats of all kinds are tied to floating docks that are attached to the seawall, and then to poles driven into the floor of the marina more than six feet below the surface.

Over the past three weeks Oscar has learned much about the man responsible for destroying his operation. His name is Grayson Cooper, and he lives on a boat in this marina. To his left Oscar sees the 43' Hatteras Motor Yacht, the name *First Draft* stamped on the stern in a font that looks like it was typed on an old-fashion typewriter. There is a set of wooden stairs on the right side of the boat about halfway up the finger dock, but he can't see an entry door from here. His men have told him that the door faces the front of the boat and he can make out the outline of it by looking through the back deck. Oscar also knows that Grayson Cooper is not a police officer, but he does some work for the local Sheriff using his own boat. As he continues moving past *First Draft*, he reaches the last building on his right and the parking lot turns slightly right, away from the marina. The pavement begins to turn back to the left toward the restaurant at the end of the parking lot and he sees a Boston Whaler sitting on a trailer backed into a parking spot on the right. The rear tires are chocked on either side with blocks of wood, a brick is holding the front wheel from moving side to side. Dust covers the boat and trailer and much of the ground around and beneath it. He can make out through the dust the name *Recovery* on the boat's left side.

Oscar passes the boat and pulls his car straight into a parking spot on the same side, the Mercedes hood ornament pointed toward a small waterway. He turns off the ignition and exits his luxury sedan. He is dressed appropriately for a marina, tan khakis and Sperry Topsiders, his guayabera shirt a nod to his Hispanic heritage. He has shaved his beard leaving only a thin mustache, his hair is cut short and stands straight up on his head.

Looking like an accountant on his day off, Oscar walks behind his Mercedes back the way he just drove in. He looks to the left out the corners of his eyes at the boat on the trailer and makes mental notes of everything that he can. He sees the repairs that look almost complete; holes in various parts of the hull are patched and sanded smooth. He is sure these are the result of his men defending themselves that night and he feels a sense of pride that he motivates men to work so passionately for him. The number of holes is astounding, and he wonders to himself, *How did this boat not sink?*

He sees the railings on the outside of the hull and wonders what those are for. His mirrored aviator sunglasses are covering his eyes so he takes out his phone and pretends to look at it, altering his path to pass closer to the boat, as though he is distracted by what is on the screen and walking in the wrong direction. He studies each part of the boat and trailer intently, hoping to understand better whether this vessel has any vulnerabilities that he might be able to exploit. Satisfied with his inspection, he looks up and begins walking to his right, turning in the direction of the marina.

He walks on the sidewalk continuing down the side of the fence that borders the parking lot. He doesn't want to bring too much attention to himself by walking on the dock itself. The sign clearly says, "Owners and Guests Only," and for now he will obey this rule. He passes a medium-sized trawler. There are bubbles coming from under the boat near the front. Looking left there is a white Chevy van backed into a parking space in-line with the trawler. Its rear barn doors are open, and a hose drops out from the back proceeding along the ground to the boat. A compressor is running noisily in the small cargo space. The van is old, late 1990s at best. The white paint no longer shines, and the graphics on the side are faded but readable; *Down Under Marine Service, We'll keep your bottom clean.* He looks back to the trawler and notices a diver just below the surface brushing along the waterline on the boat.

He looks back up and continues down the dock past a monohulled sailboat and another trawler. Oscar then sees the Hatteras sitting alone on a finger pier, the slip before it empty. At the bottom of the stairs on the pier is a mat on the dock that reads, *Welcome Aboard!* Directly across from it is a similar mat, but this one reads, *Recovery.* Again, he is studying his surroundings trying to learn all that he can and committing all of it to memory. The big boat is tied front and back to the floating dock, fenders hang from the right side keeping the boat from striking the dock itself. In the stern there are two round objects that seem to be floating in the water and look like big red rubber balls. They also prevent the dive platform from touching the dock but keep it close enough that you can step from the dock onto it.

Oscar walks past the boat and looks back at the left side now. Water is running out of a hole near the center of the boat just above the water line, and he wonders what that is for. There are other holes near the water line, but only the one is in use right now.

Satisfied with what he has learned today, Oscar turns around and begins to make his way back toward his car. As he does, a red Ford F-150 pickup truck passes him and pulls into the parking spot just behind the Hatteras. He walks past as the man is getting his things together before exiting his vehicle. Oscar turns back over his shoulder to take a look.

The man is in shorts, a t-shirt and flip flops, all of which seem to be covered in a thin film of white dust. He can see lines on the man's skin where the dust has been washed off by the flow of his own sweat. He watches as the man walks down the dock, around the right side of the boat and up the stairs onto the Hatteras. The man enters without using a key, Oscar notices. He then disappears into the vessel.

"Hello Mr. Cooper," Oscar says out loud, but under his breath. "I look forward to seeing you again."

Oscar walks back to his car, gets in and starts the engine, a plan beginning to form in his head. *This is going to be easier than I thought.* He backs out of his spot, turns the Mercedes toward the entrance and accelerates slowly back the way he came.

Chapter 5

BAM! The gunshot reverberates in the small space. BAM! BAM! Two more ring out in quick succession as I empty the last of the ten-round magazine on the Heckler & Koch .45 caliber handgun. Casings cover the floor under my feet as I lift the control lever into the safe position and set the weapon down on the shelf in front of me. On the shelf is a circular graphic, the words, *Gun Shack, Point Harbor* encircling a skull with the roman numeral, III etched in its forehead. We are at an indoor shooting range in Powell Point on the mainland just across the Wright Memorial Bridge from Kitty Hawk. I go to remove my ear protection, but Magic reaches to stop me. She shakes her head, "No," reminding me again that I am not allowed to remove them. We speak loudly to each other instead.

"What was that?" Magic asks me.

"What was what?"

"Those last two shots?"

"That was a double-tap," I say, a proud smile on my face that says, *I know the lingo.*

Magic has her finger on the button that retrieves the paper target, the outline of a human form approaching us, hanging from its left corner. It looks like a napkin suspended by a waiter awaiting your cue to place it on your lap. She is laughing and shaking her head.

"I guess that didn't work out the way I thought it would," I say.

"I hope that isn't what you intended, Coop," Magic continues to laugh. I prefer to think she is laughing *near* me and not *at* me. I know better. We remove the target and look at the result.

Overall, I did pretty well. There are nine holes in the target. One is in the white area just to the right side of the silhouette's head, three are within what would be the face, and five are in the silhouette's torso, not center mass, but close enough. Eight of the shots would kill or quickly stop any approaching threat. The tenth bullet went high and to the right, cutting through the wooden stick that suspends the target from the mechanism twenty feet down the shooting range. Knowing that the .45 caliber has a pretty good kick to it, I tried to adjust my aim to compensate for the upward movement, but I wasn't quick enough to get the muzzle back on-target before pulling the trigger again.

"Oops," I say.

"Not bad overall, but this is probably not the weapon you should be trying a double-tap with. Do you want to try my nine-millimeter again?" She asks.

"No, I prefer the .45," I say. I don't tell her it's because I can't see the bullet holes in the target when I hit it with the nine, making corrections to my aim impossible.

Two days ago, Magic began teaching me the basics of how to shoot a firearm. She has spent an hour each day familiarizing me with a couple handguns, walking me through all the safety necessary when handling one. She was surprised at my inexperience with weapons and suggested that she could teach me a few things. *I bet you can*, was my first thought. She was talking about guns though, and she has been a patient teacher. She is comfortable now that I won't hurt myself or anyone else, and this morning suggested we come to the shooting range and have a little fun. She has also mentioned that it would be a good idea for me to get my conceal carry license and to perhaps even buy my own gun. Magic doesn't come out and say it, but I think she prefers that I know how to defend myself if that need were to arise. I suppose this need is more likely now than it was just a few short weeks ago.

As a teenager my friends and I had BB and pellet guns, but we were too reckless with them for our parents to ever trust us with a true weapon. To this day I have a BB under the skin of my left butt cheek, a gift from Duke during the ninth grade. I was walking around the woods behind my house and heard leaf rustling in stereo, a *schwick* sound rapidly moving from my left to my right. That was followed by a *click, click, click* that I quickly recognized as the pumping of my Daisy rifle that I kept in the shed behind my house. I counted the pumps and when he got over eight, I started to run out of the woods and toward him. I could see he was about to pull the trigger so I jumped into the air, spinning around as though that might make a BB miss me. It didn't. Duke lowered the rifle to his hip and pulled the trigger, the BB cutting through my deck shorts and lodging under the skin of, as Forrest Gump would say, my buttocks. I went down hard, howling in pain. Duke came over, laughing his ass off. My parents asked me about my limp over the next few days, but we never mentioned a thing about it to them. To be honest, it more burned than hurt when it happened, the lingering pain like someone had punched me hard on my left glute; which I guess, someone had. Thanks Duke.

After college graduation I moved to New York City, never picking up the adult weaponry habits that are common among my North Carolina comrades. Here I stand twenty-five years later being taught how to shoot by my girlfriend. *Girlfriend.* I still like the sound of that.

"Okay, my turn," Magic says. She quickly hangs a new target from the clips and sticks a dark black bullseye the size of a dinner plate to the torso.

"What is that?" I ask.

"It's a Shoot n' See. It makes bright marks so I can see where I am hitting the target." *If I only knew*, I say to myself.

Magic pushes the button moving her target farther down range than mine had been. She seems to stop it arbitrarily and I notice it is about forty feet away. She slams a magazine quickly into her weapon. This is as familiar to her as slamming a shot of tequila once was for me.

In quick succession Magic empties her fifteen-round magazine as spent casings fly past her face, back toward me. I grab one out of the air with my right hand, thinking I am pretty cool. I feel its heat searing my skin and fling it to the floor blowing on my hand before sucking on the skin in an effort to ease the pain.

Magic turns toward me, my hand in my mouth. "What are you doing, Coop?" she asks.

"Nuffin," I respond, my hand muffling my speech.

"You caught a casing, didn't you?"

"May-pee," I say, not willing to remove my hand from my mouth. Magic shakes her head and gives me an incredulous grin. There is no need for her to respond; we both know what she is thinking.

Magic pushes the button and it seems like it takes forever for the mechanism to bring her target back to us. Mine got here so quickly. There are clearly two masses of destruction on the target, bright flourishes on the Shoot n' See. I am envious. The first mass is to the silhouette's head, the other to the center of the torso. The shots are so close together that you can't make out fifteen different holes, but instead three large ones and a couple strays just a fraction of an inch to the left and right.

"Can you make a smiley face, like Riggs?" I ask, still sucking on my hand and speaking loudly so she can hear me through the ear protection.

"Who is Riggs?" she shouts back.

I look at her with astonishment on my face removing my hand from my mouth. "*Lethal Weapon*? Mel Gibson and Danny Glover?" She shows no sign of recognition whatsoever. "Roger Murtagh, Danny Glover's character is on the shooting range with Martin Riggs, his partner played by Mel..."

"Is this a long story, Coop?" she interrupts me.

"Yes," I admit.

"Then let's discuss it another time, okay?"

I decide right then that I will rent the movie for us. She needs to be exposed to the finer things in life. I will show her the *Lethal Weapon* movies before moving on to *Die Hard*. No need to shock her system; she needs to be eased into this stuff.

"How's that feel in your hand?" she asks, referring to the HK45.

"Good. I like the weight of it. It feels like a gun should, in my opinion.

"Based on?"

"Shut up," I reply, smiling. Magic is smiling too.

Magic takes the weapon from me, making sure the control lever is in the safe position. She removes the magazine and then pulls the slide to the rear position confirming that the weapon is unloaded. She places it back into the case she brought in with her, snapping the clips into place before lifting it by the handle. We carry our ear protection back to the front desk and hand them to the man behind the counter. "Everything go well?" he asks.

"Yes, thank you," Magic answers.

"Thirty dollars," he says.

"Pay the man," Magic says to me.

"As you wish," I say mimicking another of my favorite movies, *The Princess Bride*. Magic rolls her eyes.

We walk out of the gun range. The sun is falling behind the trees to our left, the humidity a bit lower on this late summer evening. Magic stows the weapons in the back seat and then climbs into the passenger side of my truck. I have backed into the spot so turn left pulling out into the parking lot lane, then turn right out of the parking lot onto Caratoke Parkway heading south back towards Manteo.

Closer to the back of the parking lot, the driver of a small rental car waits a full minute before starting the engine. He checks his mirrors and looks around, backing into the lane, turns the car toward the exit, drives to the end and turns left, leaving the parking lot in the opposite direction.

Chapter 6

Scott Parker is running his fingers over the surface of the newly finished gelcoat, the reflection of his hand looking like a four-legged animal skating over ice. He is inspecting my work. *Recovery* is a family member to me, and I hope I have been as good a steward of her repair as the doctors were to me when they stitched me back together again. I am oddly anxious as Scott does his inspection, my finger nervously tracing the scar on the right side of my neck as he proceeds. He stops at one point bringing his face very close to the surface, as if the finishing work needs a sniff test. Apparently satisfied, he continues the manual and visual inspection.

Scott's approval is important to me. He is a former Coast Guard rescue swimmer and my partner in the contractor work we do for Dare County. He is tall, well over six feet, still built like the competitive swimmer he once was. He has a long, lean muscle mass, a massive wingspan, and big feet and hands. When his sandy blonde hair is dry it always falls forward partly covers his eyes, but on the boat, water or wind hold his hair back keeping his vision clear. I've said it before, but he looks a bit like Michael Phelps, but without the goofy grin. There is more intelligence in Scotty's eyes. He is well-educated by the U. S. Coast Guard Academy in Connecticut, and well-trained at the Rescue Swimmer Training Center in Elizabeth City, just north of here. He carries himself confidently, his body a testament to his training, his intelligent glare a nod to his education.

"Looks pretty good to me, Coop," he says in his Louisiana drawl. "I can't even tell where the scratches were."

By scratches Scott means bullet holes. He is a laid-back Louisiana boy who grew up on the northern shore of Lake Pontchartrain in a town called Mandeville. He is no stranger to getting hurt, and calls any damage done to body or property a *scratch.* As for these bullet holes, there were ten of them in the side of the hull, which I have repaired, and then two that went through the windscreen, which I have replaced. Oh, and one that went through my neck; let's not forget about that one. This, to Scott, is also a scratch, and while I can appreciate his point of view, I have reserved the right to complain about my scratch once in a while.

I think back to that night, Magic standing in the starboard bow firing on the fishing boat as automatic gunfire began to rain down on us. I look to the locations on the hull where I know the scratches – bullet holes – were. I had to dig out the remnants of each round that was lodged in the fiberglass. Had any of them gotten through, Magic would have been done. I shudder at the thought.

I thank our lucky stars – I can't seem to thank God yet – that Boston Whaler makes such sturdy boats, mine in particular. *Recovery* is a 1988 Guardian center console, twenty-five feet and powered by twin Honda 225 horsepower engines. She has a coffin box installed in the cockpit behind the helm seat, a tool of our trade; she stores the bodies we recover from the waters that surround our islands until the Sheriff's office can take possession of them. *Recovery* retired from the United States Navy in the mid-2000s after almost two decades of service. While she doesn't carry the Trident worn by others, *Recovery* is just as much a SEAL as the warriors she delivered to combat and recovered back to safety. The Guardian is a commercial vessel produced by Boston Whaler specifically for police, fire and military work. The hulls are rated to take one thousand rounds from enemy fire, and I can attest to at least ten. She is also unsinkable, as all Boston Whalers are. I found her just over two years ago abandoned in a marina yard waiting for a rescue of her own. I made a deal with the marina owner, restored her back to almost original, and repowered her with the four-strokes.

"What you thinkin' about, Coop?" Scott asks, noticing my finger tracing my scar again, an obvious tell that my mind has drifted to a different place and time. This is why I don't play poker.

I look up from the hull and see Scotty looking at me, some concern in his stare. Well, as much concern as a laid-back Cajun can muster. I return to the present and smile at him. "I'm thinking we need a shakedown trip."

"I've got the cooler. You got the keys?"

"Oh crap," I say patting myself down knowing I won't find them. "I'll be right back," I say, running the parking lot back to *First Draft*, my flip-flops sounding much like their name as I go. Scott laughs. Why does everyone laugh *near* me? I'm not willing to admit they might be laughing *at* me.

I return in my truck, backing all the way down from the Hatteras to the Whaler. Scott cranks the handle on the trailer tongue raising it a little higher as I am pulling up, then moving to the side so I can see him in my rear-view mirror. He is holding his hands about five feet apart, just over half the distance of his wingspan. As I back up, he is moving his hands closer together until finally they come together with a *slap* and he says, "Stop!"

This is the way men have worked together to hook a trailer to a truck for more than half a century. In our modern world, this is completely unnecessary. My Ford F-150 XLT has massive side mirrors and a rear-view camera that allow me to accomplish the same task with no assistance whatsoever. Scott knows this as well, but still we go through the trailer hook up protocol exactly as our Dads would have. Magic has experienced this with us before and commented that we should use the technology available to us. I questioned her logic asking her, "Why?"

"Because you can," She answered. "It's a more efficient use of your energy." Later that night I sent her flowers. It was a photo of a beautiful arrangement sent in an email. She hasn't mentioned efficiency again.

Scott disappears from my mirror stepping behind the truck. He cranks down the trailer jack until the coupler is resting on top of the hitch. A little nudge and I can hear and feel the coupler fall into place sliding over the ball. Scott lowers the jack more, the truck lowering with the weight of the trailer tongue. As all the weight is transferred to the truck, Scott pulls the pin out of the swivel mount and twists the jack until it clicks, now secured resting parallel to the surface of the parking lot. He locks down the coupler, connects the safety chains to the hooks under the truck, and plugs the four-prong wiring harness into the receptacle on the bumper. He then walks around the trailer making sure all the lights work and that the boat is strapped down for the short ride over to the ramp.

As I wait for Scotty to finish his safety inspection, I look out my windshield and notice a white cargo van in one of the parking spaces ahead of us. It's beat up as all the marine service guys vans are, but I haven't seen this one before. There are no graphics on the side, and it doesn't look like anyone is in it. My bottom cleaning guy has been slacking and I have thought about replacing him. Maybe I will stop to talk with this guy if I see him.

Scott hops in. "Ready to go," he says, pointing forward with the long index finger on his right hand. I start to roll forward. As I do, I see the apparent owner of the white van, a diver walking around its side. I know this will sound sexist, but I am surprised to see that it's a woman. She is small, maybe 5' 2", her athletic build silhouetted in her full-body wet suit. Her hair is long, pulled into a ponytail on the back of her head and then kept together with more bands down the length of it, each a couple inches apart. I imagine she does this to keep her hair out of the way while under water.

I roll up in the truck and as we reach her, lower Scott's window. "Hello," I say, trying to get her attention.

She looks up from the door of the van, smiles and says, "Buenos dia."

"I'm Coop, this is Scott. That's my Hatteras," I say pointing down the dock. "Can you give me a quote on doing the bottom once a month?"

She looks over at *First Draft*, inspecting her from a distance. "Forty-five feet?" she says, leaning her head slightly to the right and squinting her eyes, waiting for me to agree or to correct her. Her English is accented, but clear.

"Forty-three," I say.

"So close," she says, her eyes smiling, her native language causing her mouth to form a perfect circle as she says the word, *close*. It is seductive, and I think she knows it. Scott is certainly enamored at the moment. She walks over to the open side door of her van and leans in, the top half of her body disappearing into the vehicle, her wetsuit covered bottom and legs the only thing we can see. She has Scott's attention now. Who am I kidding, she has my attention too. She seems to be searching for something, her bottom half moving from side to side within the confines of the van door. Finding what she has been searching for, she stands upright, her body seeming to emerge from the van in slow motion. Her torso then reveals her head as she turns to face us, her right arm and hand still in the vehicle. Slowly she takes a step toward us as her arm and then her hand appears. She is holding a business card between her fingers as she approaches Scott's window.

"My name is Maria," she says, her tongue striking the top of her pallet as she pronounces the *r* in her name. "I am new here and am trying to build my business," she admits.

"That's okay," I reply, "It just means you'll try harder," I say with a smile. I am hoping I don't look threatening to her in any way.

She moves her right hand to her face, and then, using a finger, moves away a hair that has escaped from the bands and fallen over her right eye. She smiles back at me. Women have been doing this maneuver forever, and it always gets a reaction from men. It is having an effect on Scott, no doubt about it. It's having an effect on both of us. I stare at her.

She is younger than I first thought, maybe mid-twenties, but there is something to her that seems older, too. It's in her eyes. They give her away. There is more to Maria, something that happened to her in her life, something bad, and she is protective of it. I recognize the signs because I do the same thing.

"The first cleaning is one hundred fifty and I will check all your running gear and zincs. After that it's two dollars a foot. I can put you on a monthly cleaning all summer, basically hurricane season, and then we will spot check the other six months and see if we can't go to every six weeks or every other month."

I look at her, surprise on my face. "It certainly sounds like you have done this before," I say, smiling like an idiot. Scott chuckles because he is obviously smitten with her and he doesn't know what else to do. Smitten… that's a funny word. I think I am blushing now. What the hell?

Scott takes her card, but he can't take his eyes off of her. "Maria," he says, involuntarily.

"That's me," she responds, looking directly at him now. "Scott, right?" she says, squinting her eyes again.

"Um, yes," he replies, and then smiles awkwardly. She reaches out her right hand and Scott takes it. She shakes his hand.

"Good to meet you," Maria says.

"You too," Scott replies, forgetting to let go of her hand. He realizes that he is holding on too long and finally releases it, a look of embarrassment on his face as he looks down into his lap. I swear we have travelled back in time and I am watching Scott as a high schooler.

"Can you dive it now?" I ask.

"I have one more today and then I can come by after that."

"Works for me," I say. "Gracias, Maria."

"De nada." She hesitates a moment looking up toward the sky as though trying to recall something. Finally she says, "Coop." I feel pleasure as she says my name, her mouth again making that perfect circle. I nod my approval that she has remembered.

I begin to drive away, *Recovery* in tow. I bring up Scott's window and look over at him. Now *he* is smiling like an idiot.

"Maria, Maria, Mar-eeeeeee-ahhh," I start to sing the song from *West Side Story*.

"Shut up, Coop," Scott says, smiling like an elementary schoolboy caught holding hands with a girl during recess.

I laugh as I turn left onto Highway 64 and begin to dial the phone to fire my bottom guy. I have a new bottom girl. None of that sounds right, but you know what I mean.

Chapter 7

Magic is sitting in a wooden chair, the seat and backrest thick with foam covered in a blue and gold striped fabric, the colors of the Dare County Sheriff's office. She is on the opposite side of a massive mahogany desk shined to a perfect mirror finish. Two small flags on thin pine wooden poles – the American flag to the left and the flag for the state of North Carolina to the right – flank a black with white lettering name plaque that reads, *Sheriff Donnie Jefferies*. The man himself is sitting across from her.

Sheriff Jefferies is a mountain of a man, his massive six foot six, three-hundred-pound frame covers most of the desk chair he sits in. His chair is similar to Magic's, it's fabric and wood a match, but his is on a larger scale, a desk chair with all the moving parts that come with it, and on wheels. He is humming to himself, swiveling his seat right and left, back and forth. Magic is examining a piece of paper in her hands as he impatiently waits.

"Stop doing that," she says, not looking up from the page.

The Sheriff stops his swiveling and gets quiet. He looks at her and smiles. She doesn't raise her eyes to him, and he admires her for her balls. Very few people talk to the Sheriff like that, but he has gotten used to this kind of directness from her. He has known Zaina her entire life. When she chose the police academy over other opportunities, it was Sheriff Jefferies who had a long conversation with her India-born parents. Her mom was worried about her daughter's safety; her dad thought she could make more money being an accountant or a business manager. Both were valid concerns and so he decided to have a discussion with them about what a career in law enforcement could look like. He also promised that he would take her under his wing and direct her along the way, and in more than fifteen years he has not broken that promise. He guided her through her growth as a police officer, and now as one of his deputies, and an extremely competent one at that. She will hold his seat someday; he is sure of it. In fact, he will make sure of it.

"What are you grinning at?" Magic asks, again not looking up from her page.

"You didn't even look at me, how do you know I'm smiling," he says in his strong, eastern North Carolina accent.

"Your teeth shined in my eyes," she says, not missing a beat or looking up, hiding her own smile behind the page.

The Sheriff laughs and knows that it is probably true. After his size, he is best known for his smile. It's a smile of a politician, and he is *definitely* a politician. He has run for office six times over the past twenty-five years and has won every time. In fact, he hasn't lost an election *ever* in his life, and that includes student council president in each of his high school years. He knows people sometimes compare his grin to that of a former vice president, but he doesn't care because he also knows that the comparison stops at the smile. Sheriff Jefferies has served in this community his entire life and doesn't have aspirations to any higher office. He has been asked numerous times by his party to run for Governor and for Congress, but has each time decided to stay here where he feels more useful. A county judge position is open next year and his name has been discussed for this vacancy as well. He is considering this possibility, as long as he feels he has a good successor for Sheriff in the wings. He looks across his desk and withholds the smile he feels coming to his face.

The Sheriff leans back in his chair, swings his feet up onto the desk and sets his cowboy boots down with a *thud.* He gets no reaction. He brings his arms out wide of his body, groaning as he stretches before bringing his arms back in front of him, interlacing his fingers and resting his hands on his stomach with a grunt. Magic looks up at her mentor a look of annoyance on her face, and then laughs.

"Need something boss?" she asks.

"Well, yes Zaina, as a matter of fact, I do. Thank you for asking," he says. "I need your thoughts on that piece of paper I gave you an hour ago," he exaggerates, pointing at the page as he speaks.

Magic's look changes as concern creeps into her face, her eyes tighten a bit and she purses her lips. She finished reading it a while ago. In fact, she has read it twice and reviewed certain parts more than that. "This is troubling, no doubt about it," she says, leaning forward in her chair and setting the paper on the desk. "At least six deaths in four states that we believe are related to the human smuggling ring. Three we know are murders because they happened here, the other three are victims of a difficult passage."

"And?" the Sheriff prompts.

"And there are more that we haven't discovered yet."

The Sheriff solemnly nods. "I agree," he says as he swings his legs off the top of the desk resting his boots back on the floor. His knees underneath the desk, he is sitting straight up in his chair. He folds his fingers together again, this time his massive hands resting on the mahogany surface. He is all business now.

"And what about the guy we know only as, *Jefe*?" he asks Magic, trying to get her to dig deeper.

Magic stares at her boss. She knows what he is doing. He has come to more conclusions on his own, but he wants her to discover them for herself. He is an extremely smart man and a great teacher. *So many people have underestimated this man over the years,* she thinks. They see this massive white guy with a thick southern accent, and they make assumptions about his intelligence and ability. She is familiar with bias, although as a brown-skinned, Indian-blooded woman, her experience is different from his. She also knows that another person's bias can be used as a tool in certain situations, and they would both admit that they have often utilized it to their advantage.

Sheriff Jefferies has a bachelor's degree in Criminal Psychology from North Carolina State University, a program ranked in the top 100 in the country, and a Law degree from Campbell University in Buies Creek. While he has never practiced law, he passed the bar and has done all the continuing education necessary to keep his license current. This allows him to run for Judge in the state of North Carolina.

Jefferies saw Magic's natural talent for law enforcement and sent her to a Forensic Psychology program at St. Andrew's University in Laurinburg. While the program is similar to the

Criminal Psych program he attended, it is more specific to police investigation. Over the past year they have been working closely together, developing her skill, while exercising his.

Forensic psychology is pretty much what it sounds; you do a mental autopsy on the mind of the person of interest you are pursuing. By doing so you can determine how they think, how they make decisions, what motivates them to make those decisions and, hopefully, predict what their next decision will be. When successful, law enforcement will be one step ahead and be able to intercept a bad guy before they commit their next crime. Luckily, this part of the state rarely has a case where these skills are central to the investigation. This current case, though, is an opportunity to apply their knowledge and training.

"Jefe, Zaina?" he says again, prompting her to speak.

"I think he is pissed. I think he blames others for the disruption in his business. I think he will seek revenge on those he blames."

"Precisely," the Sheriff says, bowing his head, closing his eyes like a Sensei. "And, what else?"

"He doesn't like to lose. He takes loss very personally and attributes his loss to the individuals involved. It's not a situation that went badly, it's a person in his way."

"Agreed," he says, sitting back in his chair, a look of concern on his face.

"So you think he is going to come after me and Coop," Magic states. "How could he even know who we are? Nothing was released to the press."

"First of all, I don't think he will come after you, at least not as a primary target. He will look for the weak link and that is Coop in this case."

"In a lot of cases," Magic jokes, lightening the mood a little.

"Secondly, he *will* find out who Coop is, have no doubt about that. He thinks Coop feels superior to him because he beat him that night, and that will not stand, not on his watch," he continues. He is confident in his profile; he feels that he knows how this man thinks. He is hoping he can also determine what the man's next steps will be.

"So, what do we do?"

"We are keeping an eye on Coop when we can, but he needs to be prepared."

"I have been training him to shoot and, honestly, he is pretty good as long as his inner child doesn't channel some cop show from the nineties."

"I mean mentally prepared."

"He is," Magic says with a lack of conviction.

"I know he means a lot to you, Zaina, but we can't sugar coat this to him. He is in danger and he needs to know it."

"I'll talk with him," she says.

"Would you prefer that I do it?"

"No, I've got it," she says as she stands. "Is there anything else?"

"Unless you want to talk about the election next year, no."

"No, sir, I think that can wait," she says rolling her eyes. This gesture reminds the Sheriff of his own daughter when she was a teenager. He thinks of Zaina much in the same way.

"You are my choice to succeed me, Zaina, we need to have that conversation at some point."

"I'm not sure I am ready for that, sir."

"You are."

"I don't know how to run for office."

"You will learn."

"From you?"

"From the best, yes," the Sheriff answers showing his smile again. "To be continued… Now get the hell out of my office and do something constructive, will you?" he says, turning his attention to another file that has been lingering on his desk.

Magic leaves her meeting with the Sheriff and goes directly over to the marina. She knows that Coop is out with Scott so she can do her drive through without being discovered. She pulls down the long chute driveway until it opens to the parking lot. She drives the south side of the marina as she always does, seeing if anything looks different, or if anyone looks suspicious. Nothing today, as there hasn't been for the past two weeks. Just banged up marine service company vans taking up a few parking spots along the dock. A day in the life of Manteo, North Carolina.

Chapter 8

I push the throttles to the stops. *Recovery* jumps out of the water, the bow rising high into the air before the hull catches up with the motors. The bow comes down as it accelerates, planing off in under eight seconds. I leave the throttles at full and adjust the trim tabs until the bow finds a sweet spot and our speed increases three knots. The seas are choppy but not rough and the Whaler skims across the top with ease. Small shear waves create a slapping sound against the fiberglass hull that is the only hint the water isn't completely flat. The air moving quickly past our faces is touched with salt, the scent sparking memories of my younger days here.

I wonder how I could ever leave these Outer Banks. Running in a boat across open water as a kid is one of my most cherished memories, the sea and sun giving me life. There is a quote I love; *When I forget how talented God is, I look to the sea.* This is about as close as I get to religion these days, but that wasn't always the case. When I was a child, my church was my extended family; youth group, mission trips, fundraisers. I was involved and engaged even during my college years serving as a teen leader during the summer. Then I moved to New York for my advertising gig, and all of that changed. I lost sight of what was important, and I lost a connection to so many people that were once dear to me, and to a place that had true meaning in my life. I lost my faith.

I think of the pain I saw in Maria's eyes earlier and I am sure it is similar to the pain that I carry in mine. Over a fifteen-year period I pursued a dream that I never really had as a kid. In the advertising business though, it's what most aspire to, and so I chased it too. I was extremely successful at my job, but in the name of achievement I abandoned so much of who I was. Perhaps I started drinking because I never really liked the life I was living. It was easier than making a change, and so I almost drank myself to death on three occasions. Its different out here on the ocean though. It makes me believe that change is possible.

Traveling on the ocean carried in a sturdy vessel is a sensory experience. The horizon line in front of me has a subtle curve to it, higher in the middle, the blue sky touching the slightly darker blue sea for as far as the eye can see. The hull continues to slap on the small waves that stretch for hundreds of acres all around me. The wind created by the speed of the boat touches every piece of exposed skin moving from front to back and wrapping around my body so that I can even feel it behind me. I have removed my cap and my hair is blowing straight back, my shirt and deck shorts attempting to emulate the same attitude. I open my mouth and taste the salt tinged air.

"Earth to Coop," Scott says from my left. I look in his direction. "You may want to check your GPS," he says calmly.

I look down at the screen and see a white triangle to the right of center on the screen. I look up and to the right and see the freighter moving north. Its path and ours will cross and freighters don't like when you cross close in front of them. I turn the wheel to starboard changing our course to due south and parallel with the freighter's. I look back at the screens on my helm.

While *Recovery* was on the hard and under repair, I took the opportunity to upgrade my electronics. I now have identical sixteen-inch screens side by side on my helm, GPS on the right screen, radar on the left. On both there are white triangles at varying distances from the middle, the white triangle at the center marking our own location. Each of those triangles are the AIS signatures for vessels nearby, the Automatic Identification System used in boat traffic worldwide. Not all vessels have AIS so radar continues to be the more common way to locate other vessels. AIS, though, is a game changer.

In addition to the triangle representing the vessel on both screens, the radar screen includes information to the closest three vessels. I can see the name of the vessel, how far it is from me, what compass bearing and at what speed it is moving, and the approximate time to us being in the same location. I have had this exact setup on the Hatteras for a couple years, but I have now added it to the Whaler as well.

"That's some fancy stuff you got there," Scott drawls.

"Yes, it is Scotty," I say not taking my eyes off the screens. "The best part is that between insurance money and the Sheriff's office repair fund they didn't cost me a dime," I say, pleased with my frugalness.

"Well that is something, Coop," Scott says. He pauses long enough that I think he has finished his thought before adding, "You going to use them or just keep your nose in the air like always?"

"Fifty-fifty at this point," I admit. Even on the Hatteras I don't often use the technology I have on board. I am not a bad weather boater unless I have to be, and often my eyesight is just as good an indicator of safety as any of this will be. Still though, I like having it. If nothing else, it looks really cool. And did I mention that it didn't cost me anything?

"Help me determine if this stuff is working properly," I say.

We go through multiple steps locating vessels on one screen, then by eyesight, then on the other screen, and then comparing distances indicated on each of them. All seems to be in working order. I am amazed at how accurate the information is. While I don't often run at night, I take some comfort in the fact that I could run in complete darkness if I chose to.

"What's the latest with the investigation," Scott asks.

I look over at him surprised. "You know I'm not a cop Scotty," I say and smile brightly. Most days it's others who have to remind *me* of this, so I am taking some pride in the fact that he is asking me for an update in a police investigation.

"I am keenly aware of that Coop," Scott begins. "Your lack of skill in that arena speaks for itself, but since you are close to the primary investigator, I thought you might know something," Scott ends with his own smile. He has just upped me and he knows it. Damn that clever Cajun.

I disregard his dig. "It seems to be going slowly," I say. "Magic hasn't said much lately, to be honest."

"What about the girl?" Scott asks. He is referring to Angel, the daughter of the boat Captain who was used to compel her father, Miguel, to work for Jefe. I think about Magic's promise to him that she will find her, and her frustrations with the slow pace of the search. She keeps the picture of Angela that Miguel handed her on the top side of the visor in her department Tahoe. When she is feeling discouraged about the lack of progress, she looks at the picture, allowing her to better focus her energy. So far though, there is no information that points to where Angela might be, or if she is even alive.

"Nothing as far as I know, Scotty."

"Anything I can do?" Scotty asks.

I smile at him. This is who Scott Parker is. He has a huge heart and applies it to everything that he does. I imagine that it is what made him such an effective rescue diver for the Coast Guard.

"Actually, there is," I reply, surprising Scott.

"Name it."

"Can you keep an eye on Magic, when you can?" I ask.

He looks at me, a questioning look in his eyes. "Why is that, Coop?"

"Although she doesn't admit it, this whole situation has her stressed," I tell him. "I feel like she is protecting me, and I want to protect her."

"So you are asking *me* to protect her?"

"Well," I say, pausing a moment. "Yes."

"Okay," he says with conviction looking directly at me. "You got it."

"Thanks man," I say.

The truth is, I am very concerned about Magic. I feel that she is keeping a lot inside and I have been unsuccessful in my attempts to draw out what she is feeling. I realize that the investigation is going slowly, and I know Magic; she prefers more swift progress.

I also know that she is concerned about me. I understand why. I put on a pretty good face, but in reality, my mind is elsewhere much of the time. I can't help recalling in vivid detail the night I almost died; to be more precise, I am talking about the night a bullet almost took my life, not one of the ones where a bottle almost did. When I relive it though, the bullet hits me more center on my neck, severing my carotid artery, going through my throat and lodging in my spine. I lay there on the deck of the boat, unable to move, watching as Magic continues to fight. A bullet then passes through her body, a bloody spray covering me as her body is propelled backwards landing on the floor next to me. Her eyes are pleading with me for help, but I am paralyzed and can do nothing but watch. Her blood runs down the deck, its warmth seeping under my face as I watch her die.

I feel Scott's hand on my shoulder and look up. The fingers on my right hand are tracing my scar again. I have drifted off, Scott bringing me back with his touch.

"You okay, Coop?" Scott asks.

I hesitate before answering, "Yeah… I'm good."

"I'll do what I can, I promise," Scott says. A promise from Scott Parker is no joke. He will do what he says.

"Thanks Scott," I reply, patting his hand on my shoulder. He gives it a squeeze and pulls his hand away.

"Let's go home, Cap," he says.

I turn the boat toward shore, the line on the GPS that shows where our path will take us lining up directly with the Oregon Inlet. We pass through the inlet and then weave around the sandbars that have claimed many vessels over the years before turning north entering Roanoke Sound. Continuing under the highway 64 bridge, I turn west around Ballast Point into Shallowbag Bay. I go straight toward the historic Manteo waterfront before turning slightly south, slowing and entering Shallow Bag Bay Marina.

Producing no wake, we stay to the north of Stripers Bar & Grill into the more protected waters of the marina. About halfway down, *First Draft* is sitting at a dock to our port. There are tools of the diving trade on the dock, a white bucket with some brush handles sticking out of it, a water hose and an air hose snaking down the dock. The sound of a compressor carries over the water to our ears.

As I get close to the Hatteras, I take the throttles out of gear allowing the Whaler to slowly drift to the top of its slip. I put both engines in reverse, stopping the boat before pushing the port engine to forward. *Recovery* is well-balanced and spins exactly on her center, the stern coming around to line up with the slip, the finger pier on our port side. Scott is at midship with a line in his hand.

As the boat lines up evenly with the slip, I put the starboard engine into reverse now too, the boat moving backwards toward the seawall. I shift both engines into neutral and allow our momentum to bring us back, the breeze pushing us closer to the dock. Scott drops the line over a cleat, but doesn't hold it, allowing the stern to get within three feet of the dock before wrapping it on the cleat. I walk forward, pick up the bitter end of the bow line that Scott has left lying in the bow, and step off onto the dock. Scott does the same in the stern. We both pull the boat tight to the floating dock, fenders hanging from the pier protecting the newly finished gelcoat. We tie each of our respective lines to cleats on the dock, securing *Recovery* tight.

I look at my line, and then at Scott's. Both are tied exactly the same; once completely around the cleat, a figure eight and then a half hitch, that's it. The rest of the line is laying flat on the dock drawn into a circle called a Flemish coil. You don't need to tie a lot if you know how to tie a knot.

I look across the finger pier and there are bubbles coming out from under *First Draft*. Maria is under there somewhere, and I look over at Scott. He is also looking at the bubbles.

"Your girlfriend is under there dude," I say with a grin.

"Shut up, Coop."

I am familiar with this phrase. It is said to me quite often.

Chapter 9

A dark-haired little girl is sitting at a dining room table, a third-grade math book in front of her. Her skin is dark, her hair unkempt, long strands falling around her face. Her clothes have been recently washed, but they are wrinkled from sitting in the dryer too long. Her hair is unbrushed, but not for lack of trying. While her appearance is untidy, she has been fed well and bathed multiple times a week. She is clean and healthy.

A woman sits next to her at the table peering over the child's shoulder at the work she is doing. She is Latina, as is the girl, and their shared heritage is obvious. The woman is in her early forties though, her hair streaked with some gray and brushed back into a tight ponytail. She wears a thin floral sundress that fits tighter than it once did, its yellows and blues faded with time. She notices that the girl is stuck on the equation in front of her and asks, "Did you carry the one, Angel?"

The girl slams her pencil down onto the table, her head snapping around to face the woman. "Don't call me that!" she yells at the her. "Only my daddy can call me that!" she says pushing the book away and placing her head on the bare table.

"I am sorry Angela, but you know your daddy has to work." The woman's words are not without compassion, but Angela is tiring of hearing them. It has been months since she has seen her father. They were together on a boat coming in from Mexico and after a bad storm, she was taken from him and moved to this house. She is allowed to play outside a couple times a day, but she has not left the grounds in all the time she has been here. She is being home schooled by the woman next to her, someone she knows only as Miss Sonia.

After a couple of minutes, the girl speaks again. "Miss Sonia," Angela says, her tone much softer now, the side of her face still resting on the table. "When will my daddy be back?" she asks. She is using her sweet voice now, and using the woman's name too. These are strategies to get something she wants, a means to an end. She seeks answers and Angela knows that she is more likely to get them this way. Angela is getting worried. When she first got here, she was allowed to have a facetime call with her dad from time to time. Those calls got less frequent, and recently they have stopped completely. "I want to see my daddy," she says, her eyes welling up with tears.

Sonia feels for the girl. "When Mr. Oscar gets back later today, I will ask him if you can have a call with your papa, but first you have to do your schoolwork. Is that fair?" she asks.

Sonia strokes the girl's hair, and Angela lets her. Tears begin to fall from the child's eyes. "I guess so," she sniffles. Sonia picks up the brush and holds it in front of Angela, the gesture asking permission to use it. Angela nods her consent, and Sonia begins to brush with long strokes from the top of the girl's head to the ends of her hair just below her shoulders. "Do you promise?"

Angela asks, her tone sweet as she raises her eyes to meet Miss Sonia's. A means to an end.

Sonia is concerned about her husband. He was once a loving and industrious man. She is proud that Oscar is committed to employing fellow migrants who need assistance getting their life started in the United States. Long days and sometimes nights at the farm require workers to be there twenty-four hours a day. Her husband is also away for days at a time, sometimes more than a week. Lately, though, his mood has deteriorated to a point where they barely talk to each other anymore. She has often homeschooled a child of one of her husband's employees, but this is the first time that it has gone on for this long. Oscar has also always kept father and child connected through facetime or phone calls, but he seems to have restricted all communication between Angela and her father. This seems particularly cruel to her, and she intends on confronting him this evening when he gets back home after a week away.

"Yes, Angela. I promise," Sonia replies. While she is committed to challenging Oscar on this, keeping the promise may be more difficult. It will be up to her husband, and he has become more and more unpredictable. *What is wrong?* she wonders.

Sonia picks up the pencil Angela has been working with, hands it back to the girl and slides the book into position where she can continue her work. "Carry the one?" she questions gently.

"I did," Angela answers.

"Okay. And what do you get?"

"Eighty-nine?" she asks.

"Very good, Angela," Sonia says as she goes back to brushing the girl's hair.

There is the sound of keys in a lock, a latch being disengaged and the weatherstripping at the bottom of the door sweeping across the front floor as it opens. There is a jangling of keys hitting the small table in the entrance as the door closes again, the lock immediately latched. Footsteps are approaching them moving from the front of the house to the dining table in the back where they are working. Oscar appears in the room and Sonia can feel Angela tense up. He ignores Sonia and Angela and continues to their right to a wall that includes a with a small refrigerator beneath it. He opens the refrigerator and removes a Modelo bottle, uses the opener mounted on the wall above the counter to open it and takes a long swig. He sets a legal pad he is carrying on the countertop in front of him and begins to study it.

"Hello sweetheart," Sonia says to him.

"Hello," he replies flatly, not turning around to acknowledge her, taking another long swig and placing the bottle down on the counter with a *clunk*.

"Angela, why don't we take a break, okay?" She says, turning the girl's face so that their eyes meet. "Go to your room and read for a little bit."

"Okay," Angela says, getting up and quickly leaving the room, her body seeming to relax as she moves away from Mr. Oscar.

"What is going on with you?" Sonia says more sternly now as she stands and walks toward him. "You have been walking around here for the past few weeks spewing anger at everyone in your path."

"It's work, Sonia, it is stressful," he replies, still not looking up from his legal pad or turning toward her.

Sonia walks up behind him and touches his left arm trying to guide him to turn around, "Look at me please Oscar," she says.

He spins on her abruptly, grabbing her right arm with his hand. He glares at her, his eyes intense. Seeing his look, she tenses up and pulls away. Oscar sees fear in Sonia's eyes, and there is a sense of satisfaction in the power he feels. He also knows that he needs Sonia right now, and there are better ways to get what he needs from her. He loosens his grip on her arm, his look becomes softer.

"I am sorry Sonia," he says, pulling her closer to him and putting his arms around her. "I am trying to solve a problem that has come up."

"A problem?" Sonia asks.

"A logistical problem," he answers, his chin on top of her head. "Nothing for you to worry about. I will take care of it. I need you here."

Sonia feels his tension release, but she can't help but still feel some fear. If she is honest with herself, she often fears him. She is not allowed to go anywhere. She needs to stay right here and take care of Angela.

"Speaking of which," she says, "Angela would like to talk with Miguel." At the mention of Miguel's name, she feels Oscar's body tighten.

"That is not possible," he says, and then realizes he cannot tell her why. "He is on a trip for me and I don't know when he will return." He is looking over her head at the wall behind her, hoping she believes him. "As soon as he is back, she can see him."

"What am I supposed to tell her?" she persists. "She is getting very sad and she can't concentrate on her schoolwork."

"Tell her whatever you want Sonia," Oscar says, harsher this time, aggravation entering his tone. He extends his arms, pushing her away from him. “I have problems to solve at work, and my problems are what make us money. You can handle the little girl.” He looks down at the top of her head, but she doesn’t look up. “Now go!” he says. “I have a phone call to make!” Sonia shuffles out of the room in the direction of Angela’s bedroom.

Oscar picks up his phone and dials a number, presses the green button, and then places the phone to his ear.

After a few rings, the voice mail answers, the message from a female in English, accented slightly by her native Spanish. “Hello, this is Maria from Abajo Marine Services. I am under a boat right now, but your call is important to me. Please leave your name and number and I will call you back.” *BEEP.*

“Maria,” Oscar says, his tone divulging that he knows this is not her real name. “It’s me. Please call or text me. I want to know if you have made any contact yet.” Oscar pulls his phone away from his ear and presses the red button on the screen, ending the call.

Chapter 10

Scott opens the cooler on the dock, pulling out my Pepsis and placing them in a green cloth grocery bag with the words, *Piggly Wiggly* written across it. I keep it on the Hatteras for the rare times that I go to the grocery store. It is more often used for this purpose. I head up the steps reaching the small platform I have built there, then reach down and take them from him.

"Thank you for supporting the state of North Carolina," I say to him. Scott rolls his eyes, but he knows what I am talking about. Pepsi was invented in the city of New Bern not too far from here on the Neuse River. The Neuse is the longest river completely contained in the state of North Carolina beginning near Durham where the Eno and Flat rivers meet and running 275 miles before emptying into Palmico Sound. Heading north on the Pamlico takes you to North Carolina's Outer Banks. New Bern also happens to be the home of Hatteras Yachts, the maker of the motor yacht that serves as my home, the vessel I am standing next to and Maria is underneath at the moment. Mine, though, was built in High Point, a five-hour drive from here and from Hatteras, the town the boat-maker borrowed the name from.

Willis Slane, Jr. was a hosiery guy following his father into the High Point-based family business, Slane Hosiery Mills. The company still operates today and if you have on Nike sox right now, you can probably thank the Slane family for that. Willis the younger was also an avid fisherman, and often came to the Outer Banks for extended trips with friends. Willis was determined to build a boat that could handle the rough waters that surround Cape Hatteras, and at the time the wooden vessels he fished from seemed too light for the purpose they served. Smaller runabouts had started being built with a new material, a fabric that would be soaked in epoxy, shaped into forms, and then allowed to dry to a rock-hard finish. The new material was called fiberglass; maybe you've heard of it. Willis used it to build his first Hatteras, a 41-foot Sportfish named *Knit Wits.* The largest vessel ever made with fiberglass at the time, that boat became the standard for every boat maker at the time and since and is the foundation on which every Hatteras ever made is built upon.

When he started Hatteras Yachts he chose High Point as its home, but not just because that is where he already lived and worked. High Point is also the home of the furniture industry in the United States and it afforded unfettered access to some of the best craftsmen in the world. While the artisans and workforce were perfect for boat building, there were and are no large bodies of water near High Point, and certainly no way to transport a vessel by water out to the Atlantic Ocean. Much of the manufacturing process happened inland, and then the hulls were transported to the coast to be finished and launched. Mine has spent her entire life living in this state, and while she has wandered north and south for thousands of nautical miles, she is most at home here, and I am most at home living on her.

"I'll be right back," I tell Scott, taking the stairs to the aft deck, and then down into the Salon. I walk forward and down into the galley, opening the refrigerator and placing the Pepsi's inside. I slide the bag between the fridge and the cabinet and turn to head back to the dock. I step outside and see Maria pulling herself out of the water, Scott paying close attention.

Scott looks up at me as I step back out onto the stairs. I look down at him, make kissy lips with my mouth and pretend to hug myself. For some reason I think of a rerun of *Happy Days* where Ralph Malph does the same thing to Potsie. *Stop*, Scott mouths to me. I can't help myself. This shit is funny to me. I keep doing it as Maria sits her bottom on the dock, and then stands up looking over in our direction. I extend my arms out in front of me, and then to the side as though I am stretching.

"Oh, hi Maria," I say. "I didn't see you there." Scott leans his head to the left giving me a stare that clearly says, *you're a jackass.*

"No problem, Coop," she says, her mouth making that full round circle again, her lips pursing out as she says my name. Why does her mouth keep doing that? Why do I keep thinking about her mouth? Damn.

"How's it look under there?" I ask.

"Overall not too bad, but your zincs haven't been changed in a long time. She reaches into a pouch she has attached to a belt and removes a digital camera. Turning it toward me, she says, "See this? You need new ones on both shafts." She clicks through four photos and I can see what she is talking about. "I didn't have them with me today so I will need to get them and come back, okay?"

"Absolutely," I say. "You do whatever you need. I fired my bottom guy today." That never sounds right. "She's all yours."

"Good," she says. "I will be back tomorrow or the next day at the latest. Thank you for your business."

Throughout our conversation, Scott hasn't looked at me once. His attention is focused completely on Maria, but I also get the sense that he won't say anything and feel the need to push him in some way.

"Scott is a diver too; did you know that?" I say to Maria.

"You are?" she says, looking at him. Scott doesn't respond, he just stands there looking at her, a goofy smile on his face.

"Yes, he is," I pick up his part of the conversation. "He was a rescue swimmer with the Coast Guard."

"Wow!" she says, her mouth finishing in the round circle again. She looks truly impressed, and this brings a larger smile from Scott.

"He'd love to tell you about it some time," I continue, "wouldn't you Scott?"

This finally shakes him out of his stupor. "Um... Yes, I would."

"Well, if you give me about thirty minutes, I can meet you for a beer over at Stripers, would that be okay?" Maria says to Scott.

I can see him tense up. This is moving quickly for him and he is unsure what to do. "We are done here Scotty, you are free to go," I say to him.

"Um..." It seems that all his sentences are starting with this word now. "Okay. Sounds good."

Maria's phone rings. She reaches down into the white bucket sitting on the dock and retrieves it, an iPhone encased in a waterproof pouch. I can see the screen but from this angle am unable to read the caller ID. She gets a strained look on her face for just a moment, recovering quickly and pressing a button on the face of the phone. The ringing stops.

"Okay," Maria says, now all smiles. "See you there in thirty minutes." Scott smiles back.

Maria picks up her tools and starts carrying them up the dock to her van. Scott and I are cleaning *Recovery* and as she walks away we both can't help but follow her with our eyes, our heads turning when our eyes reach their limit.

"Getting a good look there guys?" I hear Magic's voice from down the dock in the other direction. *Oh crap*, I think.

"Yeah, Scott, you getting a good look?" I smile inside for my clever misdirection. I look up at Magic. She is leaning on the other side of the rail fence that separates the parking lot from the dock, her hands resting on the top rail, her eyes shielded behind mirrored aviators. I continue to move my head well past the direction Maria has gone. "Stretching my neck like the doctor told me to do," I say, rolling my head back and forth to illustrate the point. She's not buying it.

"Oh, you are so full of it Coop," Magic says, but she is smiling. She is dressed for work, a tan Performance Gear fishing shirt with the Dare County Sheriff logo embroidered in it, tan shorts that are longer than she wears on her days off but that still show off her fit legs, tactical boots that lace high up her shin, socks that just meet the top. I know I have described this before, but I like examining her so indulge me. She stands and places her hands on her holster, the thumb of her left hand inside the belt, her hand dangling in front. Her right hand instinctively resting lightly on the butt of her Glock 9. The sun is high in the sky, but behind her and the back light accentuates her silhouette. I have fantasies in my head that begin like this, and I think she knows it. This is her way of reminding me that she is absolutely the best thing that has ever happened in my life, and I better not screw it up. And also a reminder that she carries a gun.

"You almost finished down there?" she asks.

"Yes," I reply. "Not going to dry her today, going to leave her wet." I realize my language was probably not precise, but I have clear enjoyment on my face from the innuendo. Magic rolls her eyes – or at least I think she does by the way her head moves. Her sunglasses mask their true movement.

"Come up here if you can. I have something for you."

"Give me five minutes," I say. Magic nods and walks back to her Sheriff Department Tahoe and gets in, the vehicle still running.

"You need me anymore?" Scott asks.

"Nope, you kids go have fun."

"Thanks *Andy*," Scott says with a proud smile. I am impressed by his sarcastic reference to Sheriff Andy Taylor of Mayberry fame, especially since Andy Griffith lived right here in Manteo. I am also proud that he compared me to a real officer of the law, even if in this case real means a fictional character. Andy was still a capable Sheriff. I begin to whistle the theme to *The Andy Griffith Show* as Scott picks up his cooler and walks toward the seawall.

"See you later Coop," Scott says as he goes.

I finish spraying the Whaler down, empty the soapy water from the five-gallon bucket and rinse off the dock. I coil the hose onto its hanger on the shore power pole that is behind *First Draft*, and then drop the bucket and the yellow Shurhold brush and extension pole into the dock box next to it. The driest towel available is hanging on the railing for the stairs to the Hatteras so I pick it up and do my best to remove any standing water from my body. I look over at *Recovery*, water beading on her newly finished surface. *Leaving her wet*, I think. And then I chuckle.

I walk up the dock to Magic's truck. She points to the passenger side so I walk around the truck, open the door and hop in. If you've never been in the passenger seat of a Sheriff's truck, it isn't very comfortable. There is a computer on a mount that encroaches into the space, especially the arm space. It also blocks my view of Magic's legs which doesn't make me happy at all.

"I hope you don't text and drive," I say, pointing at the computer. Magic takes off her sunglasses and looks at me. She didn't react at all to my joke, and I know that there is something else on her mind. "What's up babe?" I ask.

Magic pauses a moment. "I got you something," she says as she spins the dials on the center console entering the combination that opens the lockbox. The top swings up towards me so I can't see inside. I'm sure there is some cool cop shit in there. Magic pulls out a black case, closes the compartment and rests the case on top. She keeps the handle toward her and slides it in my direction, the letters *HK* in red centered near the bottom of the face. *Heckler & Koch* is written in white below the letters.

She doesn't have to open it; I know what it is. It's the 45-caliber pistol that I have been working with at the gun range. I finished my conceal carry course this past week, but I didn't really plan on owning a weapon. Honestly, I shoot with Magic just to watch Magic shoot. I took the course so that I would be more knowledgeable about weapons and be able to talk about them with her. This was never about gun ownership or self-defense for me.

"I want you to have this," she says.

"I don't need…"

"Let me finish, Coop," Magic interrupts. The look in her eyes is one of concern. I nod.

Magic then explains to me what has been going on in the investigation; what they know, what they don't know, and what they believe. She tells me what they think Jefe is doing now, how he is working to find out who I am if he doesn't know already, and what his intentions will be once he has that information. I listen without interruption. When she is finished, she says, "You will probably never need it, but I want you to have it with you on the boat. I have already registered it in your name."

"You are serious," I say. It's a statement, not a question.

Magic simply nods, her eyes getting glassy as she slides it across to me. I receive the case and return her look, tears of my own filling my eyes. “I love you,” I say. It just popped out. It is the first time and I am startled by how easily they slipped out of my mouth. Normally I regret when words spill out before I think, but I don’t regret saying these three in the least.

“I love you too, Coop,” Magic says, her left hand touching my face, her thumb wiping away a tear that has escaped from my right eye. I lean in and she meets me in the middle. We kiss gently, our tears slick on our cheeks. It is the sweetest kiss I have ever experienced in my life, and as we separate, I look at her, astonished that she is with me. This powerful, intelligent, beautiful woman is my girlfriend. Girlfriend. I like the sound of that.

Chapter 11

Maria puts her tools away in the back of the beat-up van, removes her phone from the bucket and rests it on the rear bumper. She takes off her wet suit, a black one-piece bathing suit clinging to her body underneath. She carries the wet suit to the dock and grabs the first hose she comes to. She runs fresh water over the suit, turning it over before continuing, and then putting the nozzle into the neck and letting water run through the inside. She then takes the hose and runs water over her head, rinsing her hair, and then her body from top to bottom. Satisfied that she has removed most of the salt from her hair and body, she turns off the spigot and puts the hose back the way she found it. She picks up the wet suit and walks up the dock and back to the van.

Maria lays the wetsuit on the floor of the van, dabbing it with a towel. She then takes the same towel and dries her body. She slips over her bathing suit a pair of white deck shorts that accentuate her shape, and a light blue t-shirt that reads, Manteo, North Carolina on the front. She pulls flip flops from the van and drops them on the pavement, sliding each of her feet into them one at a time. She grabs her phone from the bumper and walks to the front seat.

Once sitting comfortably with the engine running and the air conditioning on, Maria looks at her phone. She sees she has a message and taps the icon.

"Maria," she hears Oscar's voice begin. "It's me. Please call or text me. I want to know if you have made any contact yet." Maria looks down at the screen and taps the icon for text messaging. She types, *I just did. I am heading to have a beer with his friend to see if I can learn more.* Thinking for a moment, Maria continues typing, *I told you I would contact you when I made contact. Do NOT call me. If you need to reach out, text only.*

She reaches up and grabs the rearview mirror, turning it toward her and studying what she sees. *Not bad*, she thinks, reaching into the drink holder picking up a lipstick stored there. She removes the top, applies the bright red to her lips, purses them to ensure full coverage and then assesses herself again. She grabs one of her business cards and kisses it, dabbing off any excess lipstick, a perfect imprint of her lips on the paper. *That will work*, she thinks.

Maria grabs her purse from the passenger seat, shuts the van off and slides out into the parking lot. It is a short distance to *Striper's* so she decides to leave the van and walk. Her path takes her behind a Sheriff's Tahoe and she notices two people sitting in the front seat. The tinting of the windows makes it difficult to see detail, but she can tell that the man in the passenger seat is Coop. In the driver's seat is a female, presumably the operator of the vehicle and therefore a Sheriff's deputy. Maria can tell that they are facing each other and involved in a conversation. She sees the female officer's arm extend toward Coop, touching his face in what appears to be affection. They lean into each other and kiss.

Feigning disinterest, Maria continues past the vehicle and around the south side of the condos and out to the dock. She walks in and sees Scott waiting for her at the bar, a Michelob Ultra sweating in front of him. He turns his head in her direction. Seeing her, he stands up, grabs the stool next to him and slides it out for her. She smiles at his chivalry, a rarity these days.

"Gracias," she says.

"De nada," Scott replies, but with a distinct Louisiana drawl to it.

"Hablas Español?" Maria asks with a smile.

"I know what that means, and the answer is 'no'," he replies, an embarrassed smile on his face.

"That's okay," she says. "I don't expect people I meet to speak Spanish," she continues, touching his right forearm with her hand. His face releases the tension that was there, and he gives her a genuine smile. He is attractive, dirty blonde hair, his right eye partially covered by its natural wave. He has a nice smile and is obviously fit, his large hand inviting her to sit next to him. He reminds Maria of someone; a swimmer she thinks, but she can't place it.

Maria sits on the stool to Scott's right and looks up at the male bartender who immediately notices her. "I'll have the same," she says, pointing at the bottle in front of Scott. The bartender slides open a cooler built into the bar, removes a cold Mich Ultra and sets it down on a cocktail napkin he has placed in front of her. "Thank you," she says.

Scott lifts his bottle and leans it toward her. "Cheers," he says.

"Cheers," Maria replies, clinking her bottle neck to Scott's, and then taking a swig of the ice-cold beer. Scott does the same.

After a moment of satisfied silence, Maria speaks first. "How do you know Coop?" she asks.

"I met him walking the docks around here actually," he says. "I had just retired from the Coast Guard and was looking at some boats. Coop was sitting on his Boston Whaler and I asked him what the name meant."

"*Recovery*?" she asks, and Scott nods. "What *does* it mean?" Maria says, her mouth making a perfect 'O' in the process before taking another swig of her beer.

"It's twofold actually," Scott explains. "First, as he would tell you, so I don't feel like I am breaking any confidences here, Coop is a recovering alcoholic."

"Really?" she says, obviously surprised.

"Yeah. He was an advertising bigwig up in New York and things got a little out of control. He needed to get out, so he moved back here," Scott explains.

"He grew up here?" she asks.

"He did," Scott replies.

"And what is the second meaning?" Maria continues.

Scott is watching her, almost studying her. His admiration is obvious. "What?" he says, not making the connection to where the conversation started.

"You said the name *Recovery* is twofold. What is the second meaning?" she asks, taking another sip of her beer.

"Oh, right," he says. "We – meaning me, Coop and *Recovery* - also recover stuff from the sea."

"What kind of stuff?" she asks.

Scott looks a little uncomfortable for a moment, but then replies, "Mostly dead bodies."

Maria it is sipping her beer as he says this and spits out a little onto the bar in her surprise. "What?" she says, placing her hand on his forearm again and looking into his eyes.

"Yeah," he says. "The Dare County Sheriff is stretched a bit thin and since most of the bodies that are in the water around here are accident victims, we help them by picking those bodies up and delivering them to the Sheriff."

"Most?" she says.

"Yes, most," he replies. "We had one a couple months back that turned out to be a murder victim… had a bullet hole right in between his eyes," Scott says, pointing his finger unnecessarily at his own forehead.

"Wow, that sounds scary," she says.

"Not really scary, but definitely different for us."

"So. what happened?" Maria asks.

"Well, Coop and Magic…"

"Magic?" Maria interrupts.

"Yeah, Coops girlfriend. She's a Dare County Sheriff," he explains. Maria nods and turns her bottle up for another drink. "Coop and Magic pursued the case and wound up uncovering a human smuggling ring."

"Wow," she says in a subdued voice. "Incredible," she continues, pronouncing the word in Spanish.

"They encountered the smugglers one night and Coop was shot in the neck." Scott goes on, "*Recovery* had holes all through her and Coop has been repairing her since. Today was a shakedown trip to see if all the repairs were in order."

"And it went well?"

"She did great."

"I'll drink to that," she says, offering a toast in Scott's direction. He returns the gesture, clinking her bottle before turning his own up and finishing what was left in it.

"Another?" Scott asks.

"I can't today, Scott," Maria says, her accent stronger now. "I have to get home and clean my stuff up. Another time, I hope?" she says, a glint in her eye.

"Yes, ma'am," Scott says, nodding his head and standing.

"Thank you for the beer, Scott," she says, placing her left hand to the side of his face, stepping up on to her toes and kissing him on his right cheek.

Scott smiles and says, "My pleasure."

Maria turns and walks to the door, her hips moving side to side as she does. Scott watches until the door closes behind her. He looks down at the bar and sees her business card sitting there, an outline of her lips on the paper with the words, *Call me* written in her hand on it. He smiles and places it in the left breast pocket of his fishing shirt.

Out in the parking lot Maria puts her sunglasses on and walks toward her van. She notices that the Sheriff's Tahoe is gone and sees Coop walking up the stairs to his boat. She is about to say something to him but decides not to. Maria takes her phone from her purse and taps in all the right places to open a text box addressed to Oscar. *We need to talk*, is all she types before tapping *send*.

Chapter 12

"They are a couple?" Oscar asks, looking out into the yard and sipping on a glass of tequila.

"Yes. She was part of the team that intercepted the boat," Maria reports. "I didn't get a good look at her though."

"Not a worry. He is the one I want," Oscar says. He turns away from the window and sits at the dining room table across from Maria. He is thinking about this *Magic* woman and any risk that she might be to his success. He must be sure that he can get

Cooper alone. The boat presents an opportunity for that. He seems to spend a lot of time alone there, at least from what he has seen and what the people who have been watching him are reporting back.

"What else?" he asks.

"He's an alcoholic," she says.

"An alcoholic?" Oscar replies, turning toward her with a look of surprise on his face.

"In recovery, yes," she says.

"Any drugs or anything?" Oscar inquires.

"Scott just said that Coop is a recovering alcoholic."

Oscar nods at this information. This presents a unique opportunity that he hadn't considered. Alcohol and drug relapses are common. He knows this because part of his own income relies on it. There are dozens of scenarios going through his mind and all of them end the same way; Grayson Cooper will be dead. He sips his tequila and sets it down on the table, grabbing a legal pad and pen. He begins to make a list of steps that will be important in the execution of his plan.

"I have to go back there tomorrow to install a couple zincs onto the shafts of his boat," Maria says.

"Zincs?" asks Oscar.

Maria wants to shake her head at his boating ignorance but doesn't dare do so. Here is a man that has utilized vessels as a central part of his enterprise, and he has never learned the intricacies of them. She wonders how he has been able to make it work; she wonders when his lack of knowledge will be his downfall.

"They are pieces of sacrificial metal that go in different places under the waterline. They protect other parts on the boat by corroding first," she explains in as simple terms as she can.

Oscar doesn't know what she is talking about but nods his head as though he understands. After all these years using boats to bring people to the Unites States, Oscar still has little knowledge of them. He hasn't needed to have the knowledge; he has relied on the Captains that he has *hired*, and the crews that work for the Captains. Going forward though, he thinks he will have to find another way. Using boats again is at the bottom of the list.

"Hi," Maria hears from the hallway to her left. She turns and sees a young girl standing there. She is wearing a pair of sweatpants that are too big for her, the garment rolled up at the waist and creating a round band around her belly. She wears a pink t-shirt with a unicorn on the front and holds a small, brown stuffed dog, cuddling it to her neck like a baby. She is barely ten years old, if that, and she is looking directly at her.

"Well, hello," Maria says, with a soft smile. She hopes one day to have a child of her own.

"Angela, go back to your room, now," Oscar says sternly. Angela looks at him, her body tensing and fear coming to her eyes. She turns and runs back down the hall.

"Is that your daughter?" Maria asks.

"Sonia is taking care of her for one of my workers," he answers, but doesn't offer any more details before going back to his list. Maria feels there is more to the story but doesn't push it. She sits watching Oscar for almost a minute until the silence gets uncomfortable.

"I have to go," she says, standing from her chair and turning toward the front door. "Did you need anything else?"

"Keep doing what you are doing," he says as he stands and walks to the window again. "Have another drink with that Scott and see what else you can learn."

Maria nods her head, but Oscar's back is to her and he cannot see it. She feels a surprising stir at the mention of Scott's name. This man is a source of information, she needs to remember that. She has to admit though, she finds herself thinking about him. His good looks, his body. She thinks about how he stood and pulled her chair out when she arrived. He obviously respects women, unlike the man standing in front of her.

"I can do that," is all she says before walking out the front door.

Chapter 13

I step down from the aft deck to the salon on *First Draft* and walk across the small space to the counter that divides salon from galley. It also doubles as my writing desk. I place the gun case on top of some papers strewn there, my handwriting illegible across many of the pages, my laptop siting unopen next to them. These are the tools of what I hope to be a new chapter in my life, one as a writer of fiction. I was making great progress on my first book until something happened a couple months ago. What was it? Oh, I remember; I was shot. I spent almost a week in the hospital, and since arriving back here to my home I haven't written a single word. Writer's block is real.

I look down at the case and open it revealing the Heckler & Koch HK45 pistol inside, an empty magazine resting in the black foam cutout next to it. Magic has placed inside the case a box of 45-caliber ammunition as well. I lift the pistol out of the case wrapping my fingers around the grip holding it in my hand. It truly does feel good to me, but odd at the same time. This is the first time I have ever held a weapon outside of the shooting range and as much as I play cop in my head, having an actual gun in my hand on my boat – in my house – feels strange.

The gun is entirely black, its matte finish hiding any surface inconsistencies that might exist. The parts are well-oiled, and the pistol is ready for use if need be. I set the weapon back into the case, removing the magazine and ammo, opening the cardboard box and allowing a handful of cartridges to spill into the case. I click ten rounds down into the magazine. On television when you watch people do this it looks so easy. It's not. The first time Magic had me load the weapon I kept dropping rounds on the floor because I couldn't seem to combine the pressure it took to get them in with the precise location on the magazine. It takes quite a bit of force and perfect placement of the cartridge to get it loaded. I am a bit more skilled at this than I was then, but still two bullets end up on the floor under my chair. Once finished, I lift the gun again, slide the magazine into the grip and make sure the control lever is in the safe position.

I lift the weapon like Magic has taught me, looking down the barrel and lining up my refrigerator in the site. It is only four feet away and I am pretty sure I could hit the spot I am focusing on from here. That magnetic pen holder wouldn't stand a chance. I think back to target practice on the range, aiming and shooting at the printed black outline of a human being. Standing here in my salon aiming at an object that I use every day is disconcerting. I can't imagine if it were an actual living person standing in front of me. Could I shoot someone? I honestly don't know. Just thinking about it makes me very uncomfortable. I don't like it.

I eject the magazine and place it and the HK back into the case. I look around the boat and wonder where to store it. In the sea adventure books that I read all the main characters are comfortable with guns and have multiple weapons hidden in secret compartments around their boats. I have none of that but vow to create something soon. I step down into the galley, remove the Piggly Wiggly bag that is next to the refrigerator. There is just enough space between the fridge and the cabinet, and I slide the case in, replacing the green bag on top of it, concealing the gun case as best I can. I stand and look down, inspecting my work. The pig's face on the bag is looking up at me as though he is saying, *great hiding place, dumbass.* It will have to do for now.

I exit the salon stepping up to the aft deck, then continuing around to my left and up to the helm station. I walk over to the console and unfasten the snaps holding the white Sunbrella cover in place, remove it and set it aside on the port side bench seat. I turn the starboard engine ignition key to *ON* and hear the familiar high-pitched screech. I mash my finger on the start button and the engine begins to turn; three seconds later I hear the engine fire up and the high-pitched alarm go silent and I release the button. I do the same with the port engine before walking out to the dock to check water flow through the engines. The Detroit 671 turbos are smoky, but that will clear as they warm up.

I head back up to the helm and open the hatch on the starboard side revealing a breaker box. I turn each of the switches on, close the hatch and go back to the helm. Leaning against the seat I remove the covers from each of the electronic screens and notice that they are already turned on and are cycling through their boot-up procedures.

The monitor to port is set for radar. The screen is mostly black but has five white, concentric circles extending out from the center. The smallest circle represents two miles from the center of the screen, which is the location of the boat. Each circle around it is two miles farther away from the previous one. Radar isn't spinning so there are no blips on the screen. I know *blips* is a scientific term but suffice it to say that if there were any, they would represent other vessels or some type of navigational aid. There are, however, white triangles on the screen, including one almost on top of the center of the screen. I look to the right side of the screen to see the vessel information on the AIS. It says, *Recovery*. I look over toward the Whaler realizing that I left the electronics on after our shakedown run. I step down from the helm and off the Hatteras, cross the finger pier and step on to *Recovery*. Standing at the helm I lift the covers from each screen, and both are still turned on. I have the electronics set up exactly the same way as the Hatteras, so the left screen reveals an image that is almost identical to what is next door, a white triangle almost sitting on the center of the radar. Looking over to the right the vessel information this time says, *Mary Elizabeth.* I remind myself that I need to register *First Draft* with the FCC so that the AIS locator information has the right boat name. It is still broadcasting the name given by the Hatteras' previous caretaker.

I turn off the screens and then go to the electrical panel and click off the switches for Radar, GPS and AIS. I remind myself to turn all of this off next time. I know this won't be the last time I make this mistake; remembering stuff isn't one of my strong points.

I head back to the Hatteras. The Detroits have settled into their slow roll, the subdued guttural roar telling me they are ready to go if I am. There is a light mist of exhaust smoke drifting behind the boat, the earmark of an old diesel engine, the smell of the spent fuel in the air. I check the systems on the helm and all are operating as they should. I look at the gauges for each engine and all are within the ranges they should be while idling at the dock. I can't help but think how enjoyable going for a ride with a beer and a cigarette would be right now, but I don't dare go there.

I reach back into the breaker box on the starboard bulkhead and turn off the electronics. Standing at the wheel, the screens are now dark. I press the STOP button on the port engine until the

RPM gauge reads zero and the alarm sounds. I turn the ignition key back to its up and down position silencing the alarm, and then repeat the same process with the starboard engine. I put the helm cover back in place and step down onto the aft deck.

Scott is approaching from the direction of *Striper's*, a smile wide across his face and holding a Michelob Ultra in his hand. Over the din of life at a dock I can hear him humming a song to himself. Is that Bobby McFerrin *Don't Worry Be Happy*? I almost laugh out loud. I am glad to see him like this though. He deserves it. I think back to telling Magic that I love her, and I smile too. Whether I deserve it or not is a discussion for another day.

As Scott approaches, I throw him a *First Draft* koozie and say, "Put that on your beer man!" He catches it in the air and slides the wet bottle into it. I continue, "Oh, and you left the electronics powered up on the Whaler."

"It's your boat Coop," he says, still smiling and taking a sip of his beer.

"Your first mate. It's your job to remind me," I say.

"Whether I remind you or not you probably won't do it," he says. He's not wrong. I can sometimes be a poor listener. Okay, most of the time I am a poor listener. What was he saying?

"So?" I say, an obvious request for information.

"'So', what?" he asks, but he knows what I want to know. I will have to drag it out of him.

"The drink? Maria? Don't make me sing again."

As I am about to break into song, he holds his hand up to stop me. "It was good. She is very nice."

"What did you talk about?" I ask.

"I honestly don't remember Coop," Scott says. He is looking up into the sky as though the answer might be there. He gives up and looks back at me. "I enjoyed her company," he says. "She was sweet, and she drinks beer." I understand how important that is… better than he knows.

"Well, good," I say. If I had a drink I would lift it toward him in a toast. In lieu of that, I raise my empty hand. He does the same with his bottle, mimicking clinking it to my imaginary one.

"Now get back to work and don't forget to remind me to turn off the electronics next time," I say.

Laughing, Scott says, "Screw you Coop." He walks away down the dock back toward the parking lot.

Chapter 14

Beep... beep.... beep... The sound has an even cadence to it, a high-pitched metronome without an instrument to accompany it. The screen it resonates from displays a jagged line across it, a small spike up before a large one, then a large spike down before a small one. These are the marks of a heartbeat, blood running through a body keeping it alive. The monitor regulates only the pumping of the heart, not its ability to do so on its own.

There is a gasping sound coming from another piece of equipment in the room, the sound followed by a low rumble for a couple of seconds, then another gasp. The respirator is connected to a tube running into the patient's mouth, down his airway and into his lungs. It fills a body's lungs with oxygen before allowing the weight of the chest cavity to push the air back out of the body.

Another screen rests atop an aluminum pole, a four-point rolling stand on the floor supporting it. The markings across the glass screen resemble writing paper handed out in elementary school, as though a child could work on their penmanship by writing between them. The electronic lines on this screen are nothing like those on the heart monitor, though. Where the heart monitor has life to it, the lines on this screen do not; multiple lines extend left to right across it, not one showing a ripple of activity. This is the brain scan of the man laying in the bed in the center of the room. Magic sits next to him reading aloud from *Captiva Breeze*. Miguel – the patient – is a Captain and she thinks he would love the stories told by Ed Robinson, one of her and Coop's favorite authors. Perhaps he can even relate a bit to the main character, Meade Breeze, a good man who often finds himself in ethically complicated situations.

A doctor walks into the room and Magic pauses from her reading and looks up. He is a slight man, not more than five-five and a hundred and thirty pounds. His black skin is in sharp contrast with his white lab coat, his bald head making him look older than he is. "Hey Spence," she says, looking up at him. "How's he doing?"

"Hello Magic," the doctor says recognizing she is in the room for the first time, no emotion in his eyes. He does more work before continuing. "He is the same as always. His body is being kept alive by machines, and his brain is not functioning whatsoever."

"Don't sugar-coat it Spence, tell me how it is," Magic says, a smirk on her face. The doctor continues his inspection of patient and paperwork and pays no attention to her. Magic is used to this from Dr. Spencer Washington.

Spencer is a savant. At only twenty-seven he has been practicing medicine for more than five years. He graduated college when he was just fourteen, attended medical school in his late teens and had completed residencies in New York and Washington, DC by the age of twenty-one. As a young man in his native Greensboro, North Carolina, he was diagnosed with Asperger's Syndrome, both a blessing and a curse for Doctor Washington.

The hyper focus on certain topics that comes with Asperger's is certainly part of his success in the medical field. But as a slight-in-stature young black boy growing up in the south, bullying started early. Add to that his difficulties in social situations and the fact that he was younger than the typical student at Western Guilford High School, Spencer became the target of bullies who vented their own insecurities by tormenting him. Luckily though, Spence's inability to read facial expressions kept him largely unaffected, and his focus remained on school and on a future in medicine. Until a student yelled at him.

The sound of a person yelling changes Spencer Washington. As slight as he is, the bully who chose to yell into the aspiring doctor's face immediately regretted doing so. Always one of the shortest kids in the class, Spence's head came only to the boy's chin. Also, the bully had stepped so close to Spencer that one of the shorter boy's feet was positioned directly in between those of the bully. As soon as the bigger boy started shouting into his face, Spence flinched, attempting to protect himself by contracting his body into the fetal position. By doing so, he raised his knee into the bully's groin with tremendous force. At the same time Spencer raised his elbows above his head, part of the involuntary protective response. The actions resulted in lifting the boy into the air by his privates, and then slamming him to the ground head-first by driving his elbows under his chin. The boy also bit his tongue. Spencer uncoiled and, no longer seeing or hearing anything threatening, walked to his next class. He was twelve.

Mainstream school was no longer part of Spencer's life after what his parents call, *The Incident*, and he finished high school, and then college in the next two years. To this day he shows little to no emotion, so while he is a very well-educated and talented doctor, his bedside manner is lacking.

Without making eye contact, Spencer continues in his flat tone, "If family were here and he wasn't part of a police investigation, we would have let him go already."

Magic looks over at Miguel unable to hide the sadness in her eyes. Spencer finishes the work he has been doing and raises his head toward her, a blank look on his face. He makes eye contact for just a moment, but again looks away before speaking.

"He had no blood going to his brain for a long time. People don't recover from that," he says.

"Never?" Magic asks.

"No, not never," he admits. "Statistically the number is almost zero," he says in an almost mechanical voice. "We have done everything we can for him and without the aid of these machines he would almost certainly die."

Magic appreciates his direct language and knows he isn't lying; Spencer is unable to lie. "I'll talk to the Sheriff and see what he wants to do. We would love to be able to talk with him one day, but keeping him alive like this..." Her words trail off and she doesn't continue the thought.

"Do you need anything else from me?" Doctor Washington asks, his eyes inspecting something on the ceiling in the corner.

"No," Magic says. Thank you, Spence."

"You are welcome," he replies, his voice without emotion, before turning and walking out of the room.

Magic stands up from the chair she has been sitting in and takes Miguel's hand in hers. She looks down into his face, inspecting the lines around his closed eyes. The first time she saw this face he was sitting in the Captain's chair on a fishing boat, a storm raging around the two of them. Magic immediately aimed her gun at him and demanded that he put his hands where she could see them. Miguel's hands were across his stomach and, lowering her flashlight to reveal what they were doing, she saw the blood leaking out through his fingers. He was bleeding badly from a wound just under his rib cage, his blood pooling with rainwater on the deck. As she tried to administer whatever aid she could, Miguel used his remaining strength and removed a picture from his breast pocket. "Find her," is all he could say. Looking into the eyes of the young girl in the picture she knew immediately she was his daughter. The eyes in the picture had more hope in them, but they were the same as the man in front of her. She promised Miguel she would find her, and she hasn't forgotten that promise.

Since that night Magic has been able to identify his daughter as Angela Cortez, but so far has been unable to get any leads as to where she could be, or if she is even alive. At the time, Miguel was the Captain of the vessel that served for so many as the illegal entry point into the United States. He didn't do it willingly though, he did it under duress. His daughter was being held from him until he finished out his contract. As he lays here, Magic can't help but wonder if he knows what is going on around him.

Hoping he can, Magic leans in close to Miguel. She places her hands on either side of his face and quietly says, "Stay with us Captain. Your daughter needs you." She picks up her book, turns and walks out the door of the room. As she does, she wipes a tear from her eye.

Chapter 15

The sun to the east is still low on the horizon, its glow creating a path on the water of the channel, a yellow brick road of sorts. This one leads out to the bay, and then to the Atlantic Ocean, its own version of Oz. The air is cool, a hint of the fall that is just around the corner. The scent of salt air is enhanced by a waft of coffee steam coming from a mug that reads, *Captain*, sitting in front of me. I am at the helm seat on the flybridge, my feet crossed right over left, barefoot on the console.

I love mornings now, but that wasn't always the case. When I lived in New York City and worked in the advertising business, my workdays were long, leading to late dinners and drinks often ending with me drunk and stumbling home in the early hours of the next day. And by *often*, I mean *always*.

Heading to work the next morning was a chore. I would step out of my Murray Hill condo onto East 39th Street and turn left, grabbing my first cup of coffee from a street vendor at the corner of Park Avenue. My body cast a long shadow on the sidewalk in front of me and I would hold up my cup into the light and study the way the steam cast a shadow as well, albeit fleeting. I was thankful that my walking commute headed west; the sun in my eyes would have proven too daunting and deterred me from going to work at all.

Coffee was a tool for me then. It woke me up enough to get me to work, and then multiple cups throughout the day kept me going by slowly adding blood to my alcohol stream. To hide the smell of the alcohol seeping from my pores I wore a significant amount of cologne, so it was impossible for me to truly smell the coffee.

Today I sit here at the helm of a boat as the sun rises, cherishing my view, the scent of the coffee-tinged air and the taste of the warm liquid in my mouth. I do this every morning, rain or shine, under the cover of the flybridge. How far I have come. How far I still have to go.

"Got a cup up there for me Captain?" I hear Magic say from the dock. Her voice is a welcome addition to my day, and I think about how lucky I am at this moment in my life. Maybe I have come farther than I give myself credit for.

"There is a mug with your name on it sitting next to the pot in the galley," I say not moving from my perch. "Would you like me to get it for you?" I ask, secretly hoping she says, 'No.' I am pretty comfortable where I am.

"No, I'll grab it and be right up." *Whew.*

I wait as she goes below, and then comes up to the helm, steam coming from her Orlando Magic coffee mug. I said it had *her name* on it, not *only* her name. I found the mug at the Goodwill in town and I had to get it for her.

"Thank you for my mug," she says, her mirrored aviators serving as a headband harnessing her long, dark hair, her eyes glassy as she kisses the side of my head. "This is so sweet," she continues, admiring the mug as though it is a piece of jewelry. I am going to be honest; I bought the mug because I thought it was humorous, and that we would have a laugh about it. Apparently, though, I did something very – and I am quoting here – *sweet.* Admittedly, I am poor at *sweet,* so I am confused as to what I did that qualifies as such. I am determined to unravel this mystery though; if I have any hope of repeating it – and getting the reaction from Magic that I am enjoying now - I am going to have to figure this out.

Magic sets her mug in the holder on the helm, steps close to me pressing her right hip against my left thigh, and then leaning in and laying her body against mine. She puts her hands behind my neck and pulls me closer to her as she rests her head in the place between my shoulder blade and my shoulder. This gets me every time.

I slide my sunglasses up so that she can see my eyes, and I look down toward her face. Her eyes are glassy, and I start to wonder how many Orlando Magic items there might be in Manteo, North Carolina. I will get her every one of them. Her mouth is close to my neck and I can feel her warm breath when she exhales. Her chest expands as she takes her next breath, her lungs fill with air, her breasts pressing harder against my body. I am not sure what the intended affect is, but I am predictable. Every part of my being is moved, some parts more than others.

I set my coffee aside and wrap my arms around her, resting my face against the hair on the top of her head.

"You okay, Magic?" I ask.

She stays where she is for a few seconds, a pause before she begins. "I visited Miguel last night," she says.

"Any change?" I ask, already knowing the answer.

"No," she replies anyway. "I have a meeting with the Sheriff later this morning to discuss what we should do."

"Do you mean about keeping him on life support?"

"Yes," she says, raising her head and looking at me. "It feels selfish at this point. I want him to wake up. I want him to be able to see his daughter again. More than that, I want Angela so see her dad again."

I don't reply. Instead I stay silent and wait for her to say what she really wants to say.

She rests her head back to that special spot. "I can't find her Coop. I have nothing," she says finally.

"You will," I say.

"I won't," she resists.

"You will."

Magic stands again and looks into my eyes. "How can you be so sure? You almost make me believe it, regardless of the fact that I have absolutely nothing."

"Magic, you will find her. You won't give up until you do. It's who you are." She rests her head into my neck again and I hold her tighter. "When I was in advertising and I couldn't seem to come up with an idea, I would try something."

"Drinking?" she says with a laugh.

I smile. "Well, yes, but that isn't what I am talking about," I say as I poke my finger into her ribs. Magic is ticklish and she pulls away with the giggle of a teenage girl.

Standing in front of me she says, "So what is your secret Obi Wan." I love her even more for her galactic reference.

"I say it out loud."

"Say what out loud? That you will write?"

"I would say out loud to the universe that I would succeed," I said.

"Were you drunk when you did this?" she says through a smile.

I pause a moment. "Well, probably," I admit. "But that doesn't make it any less applicable."

"So, I should tell the universe that I will find Angela, is that what you are saying Coop?" Magic asks, skepticism in her voice.

"Exactly," I reply confidently. "Have you ever seen the movie *Dead Poet's Society*?" I ask.

"Are we going to do this again?" she asks, exhaustion in her voice. While not an impassable divide, our ten-year age difference is apparently eras in pop culture.

"In that movie…"

"Here we go."

"In that movie," I continue, talking over her, "Robin Williams makes a student, played by Ethan Hawk, *YAWP! barbarically* in front of the class. The exercise shows the student that he has an ability to write poetry."

"First of all, love me some Ethan Hawke," Magic starts, a mischievous grin on her face. "Secondly, that is from a Walt Whitman poem. *'I sound my barbaric yawp over the roofs of the world.'*"

"Exactly!" I say, not hiding how impressed I am that she knows this, but also not showing any surprise. I am amazed by Magic regularly.

"I will find Angela Cortez," Magic says unenthusiastically.

"Not like that, you won't," I say.

"I will find Angela Cortez!" she says louder now.

"Convince the fishermen off the coast!" I push farther.

"I will find Angela Cortez!" Magic says loudly while laughing and hugging me. She looks into my eyes, and then places her mouth firmly on mine, kissing me deeply. I am about to suggest a change of venue when we are interrupted.

"Who is Angela Cortez?" I hear Maria's voice say from the dock. Magic laughs and lowers her head into my chest, probably thinking the same thing I am; *horrible timing*.

Magic walks to the edge of the flybridge and looks down at Maria. "And you are?" she asks Maria, knowing full well who she is.

"Oh, I am Maria," the *r* sounding like a *d.* "I am doing bottom cleaning for Coop," she says.

"I bet you are," Magic says to me out of the corner of her mouth. I smile. She turns back toward Maria and says, "Just something I am working on."

I walk up behind Magic and peer out over the edge of the flybridge. "What brings you out here, Maria?" I say, trying but failing miserably at an accented pronunciation. I can feel Magic trying not to laugh.

"I have the new zincs. I was going to install them if that is okay," Maria says. "I can come back if that is better."

"No, that's okay. I have to get going," Magic says. I let out a sigh that isn't nearly the release I was hoping for this morning.

"It's all good," I say to Maria.

"Okay," Maria replies, her mouth making that round shape again. Damn, this morning is getting frustrating.

Magic looks back at me, not hiding her laughter any longer. "What a lucky find for you Coop. I'm sure she is an excellent bottom cleaner."

Ignoring the insinuation, I say, "She really is. She takes videos and pictures under the boat to show me how it looks."

"So, she has a nice bottom then," Magic says, baiting me.

"If you are talking about *First Draft*, then yes, she has a very nice bottom," I answer carefully. "A nice, curved, clean bottom," I continue looking off into space, pushing my luck.

Magic punches me in the ribs, but she is laughing. "Careful now Captain. I carry a gun, remember?" How can I forget? It turns me on every time I think about it.

"I have to get going," she says. "I'm meeting Jefferies at ten."

"Okay," I say, kissing her on the lips, lingering a bit, hoping to slow her departure. She pushes away slowly, turns and starts down the flybridge stairs. "Nothing?" I ask.

Magic laughs as she steps out the aft deck door onto the dock steps. She looks up at me and says, "I had to get moving in this direction or I wouldn't want to go," she says giving me an ego boost. This is high praise to me.

"Dinner tonight?" I ask, inuendo dripping from both words.

"I can't," she says. "Jefferies wants to discuss his succession plans with me and a consultant tonight. We are going to dinner at 1587."

"Nice place," I say.

"Well, since you don't take me there..." she continues, leaving the rest unsaid. She is teasing me, I know, but I can't help thinking that this is probably one of those *sweet* things that I am poor at. I make a mental note.

"Are you considering a run for Sheriff?" I ask. We have discussed this but so far Magic has refused to commit to her boss' succession plan.

"I guess I am," she says, looking up at me. "You okay with that?"

"I am," I say, a big smile on my face.

"Why the grin, big boy?" Magic asks.

I am full of pride, but instead I say, "Because I am going to sleep with the Sheriff of Dare County." I do a little dance that I am sure looks nothing like the happy dance it is supposed to be.

"I'll tell Jefferies to watch his back," she says. Damn, she is quick.

"Well, he is a handsome man," I say, smiling. "But he's not my type. Not that there's anything wrong with that," I say in my best Jerry Seinfeld.

Magic looks at me, a puzzled look on her face. "*Seinfeld*?" I ask.

"Never saw it," she says as she turns and walks down the dock.

I really need to educate this woman on the important things in life.

During the exchange between Coop and Magic, Maria is sitting on the dock preparing to dive under the Hatteras. She takes her time and even fumbles a few steps. She feigns disinterest in the conversation happening above her, but she is paying close attention to every word. Ever since hearing the little girl's name, she hasn't been able to focus on anything but their conversation. She vows to find out more, but right now there is important information she needs to pass on.

Maria picks up her phone and pulls up Jefe's number. She types quickly, and then presses SEND. She waits a moment to be sure the text message is delivered. The words she typed move from the dialog box to a green bubble just above it, and read:

He is alone on the boat tonight.

A green check mark appears next to the words. She deletes the message and returns her phone to the waterproof pouch, and then to a pocket in her wetsuit.

Chapter 16

There are still a couple hours of daylight, but I am getting hungry. I don't normally cook for just one person so I grab my wallet and head out to the dock, and then to my truck. I look down at my Hatteras, the low sun lighting up the port side like she is the subject of a photo shoot. *First Draft* is a pretty vessel. I think about going back to the boat and ending the day with a drink on the flybridge. Unfortunately, this is something I cannot do. Instead, I start my truck and pull out of the marina, drive over the bridge to Manns Harbor and turn left into the parking lot of *Duke's*

Diner. I shut the engine off, step out of my truck and saunter over to the restaurant and open the door.

"Do you ever eat at home?" is the greeting I get as I walk in. My childhood friend is referring to the fact that this is the second time today that I am eating at his establishment. I eat here a lot, but it is rare that it happens two times in the same day.

"I'm the kind of guy who likes to live on the edge," I reply.

"*The Sure Thing.* I love that movie," Junior says.

"Exactly!" I say as I hold my hand up for a high five. I am celebrating the fact that someone understands one of my movie references.

"What are you doing?" he asks.

"High fiving you."

"No, you're not."

"Why not?" I ask, dejection in my voice, my hand still in the air.

"I don't high five," he says. I had forgotten this.

I lower my hand and make a fist. "Fist bump?"

"Even worse," he says.

By this time, I have attracted the attention of the crowd, half looking on with a little bit of fear in their eyes, the other half having a good laugh at my expense. I notice it's the people who know me best who are laughing.

"Sit at the counter, Coop," Junior says. "I'm saving booths for couples or more. Did she finally come to her senses and leave your ass?" he asks.

He has guessed that I am alone; my second time in one day was an obvious clue, but I am also wearing my favorite ECU t-shirt. When I wore it the first time it was a glorious Pirate purple with *ECU* in bright gold letters across the front. That was more than a couple decades ago when I was still a student at East

Carolina University. Today, the purple is faded, almost a gray with hints of blue in it. The screen-printed letters are cracked but still hanging on and readable. A hole has formed in the seam on my right shoulder, and there is another just to the left of my navel where the fabric has simply given away.

I do not wear this shirt in the company of Magic. She says it is too old, and that I look homeless when I wear it. I point out that I live on a boat, and there isn't a huge leap to homeless from there. She is embarrassed to be seen in public or at home with me wearing it, so I keep it for special occasions like today. At other times the shirt is well-hidden from view. If it weren't, I am sure that Magic would have made it disappear already.

Duke slides me a tall, plastic cup filled with Pepsi and ice. "The dinner usual," he asks.

I stare back, a hurt look on my face. "Do I look like a *usual* kind of guy?" I ask.

"Yes."

I pause a moment, looking up at him, trying to think of something clever. "Okay, the usual," I surrender. I've eaten the same dinner here since we were in high school, meatloaf, mashed potatoes and okra. I have dinner here at least once a week since coming back to Manteo, so after being absent from this establishment for fifteen years or so, I am making up for lost time.

Junior doesn't do the meatloaf like his dad did, though. His dad used to bake a large loaf of ground beef and then serve slices on a plate with a pile of ketchup next to it. Junior makes individual loafs, basically large hamburgers with some secret flavoring mashed into the mix. He then rolls each loaf in ketchup and spices, sears the outside in an iron skillet, and then puts them into the oven at four hundred degrees to a customer's preferred temperature. The mashed potatoes are lumpy, and I used to make fun of him for it. He does this on purpose and has said forever that they are better this way. He is right, but I won't ever let him know that. The okra is fried like it is supposed to be, and just salty enough to make the Pepsi taste sweeter.

Junior comes out of the kitchen wiping his sweating bald head with a white rag. "So where is your much better half tonight?" he asks.

"She is having dinner with Jefferies and a political consultant."

"She's gonna' do it, isn't she?" he says with a smile that is in contrast to his booming, gravelly voice.

"That's what they are talking about tonight," I confirm.

"You okay with that?"

"Completely," I answer. "She is an incredible deputy and she will be a great Sheriff."

"I agree," Junior says, smiling. "I just wonder if it doesn't intimidate you that she wears the pants in your relationship."

"I wear deck shorts and flip flops, so someone has to," I say, pointing to my Billabongs and Olu Kais.

Truth be told, I have some reservations about Magic running for public office. At the ad agency in New York we periodically did work for candidates, and it is a dirty business. So much time is spent reviewing *opposition research*, a type of research designed to uncover unsavory parts of an opponent's life. Nothing is off-limits; Halloween costumes in high school, comments secretly recorded at a fundraiser, family members and their behavior, and significant others, past and present. It's that last part that worries me. An alcoholic boyfriend who earned much of his money as a settlement in an HR dispute is not typically an asset to a political candidate. And it will come up, no question about it.

Junior sees the concern on my face. "I'm kidding man, you know that."

"Oh, I know," I say, shaking away my thoughts and returning to the conversation. "I was just thinking about the public scrutiny she will get."

"You sure you aren't worried about the public scrutiny *you* might get?" Damn, he can read right through me.

"I am not worried about me; I'm worried about her. I am not exactly the ideal partner to have in a political race."

"Dude," Junior says, shaking his head and leaning down to the counter, "for whatever reason – and whatever that reason is, it eludes me – Magic loves you. She is aware of your faults; she is aware of your past. And I'm sure it will be the topic of conversation through the campaign. But I am also sure that she wants you there."

I look up at my lifelong friend. This might be the nicest thing he has ever said to me. "Are we supposed to kiss now, Number Two?" I ask, my ability to deflect serious conversation coming on in full force.

"Fuck you, Coop," he says with a smile, standing back up and snapping the rag in the air in front of my face before walking back to the kitchen.

I finish every bit of food on my plate, wipe my mouth with the napkin from my lap, and then place it on the counter in front of me. I drink down the rest of my Pepsi and put a twenty-dollar bill down, setting the plastic cup on top of it. I grab a pen and napkin from a holder behind the counter but within reach, and scribble a note, turning it over and placing it with the twenty.

"I'll see you Junior," I shout to the back of the kitchen, slapping the counter twice with my hand as I stand and walk out the door. I stop and look back in through the window as Junior comes out of the kitchen to where I was sitting. He takes the twenty and then picks up the napkin, turns it over and reads what I wrote. He smiles, folds it up and places it in the small front pocket of the apron he wears.

As much as we rib each other, Junior and I are both sentimental types. We have for decades been tough in front of others, but always complimentary and supportive of each other in private. I guess that is a guy thing; be supportive to another guy, but don't let others know about it. Junior was a big reason I came home after getting sober. I knew I had at least one person who would be supportive of me, but who would also not patronize me or pussy-foot around things. Long ago I apologized to him for the negative impact my drinking had on our relationship, and long ago he forgave me.

Junior walks over to the register and places the twenty inside before closing the drawer. He reaches back into the small pocket on his apron and takes out the note I left. I can see it from outside, a small, white memo with writing that runs up one side, and then turns with the angle of the napkin proceeding down the edge of the other side. I can't read it from here, but I don't have to. I wrote it. *Thanks for being in my corner*, it says.

I turn and walk to my truck, hop in and start the engine. I sit a moment, pondering my life. Again, I can't help but think how lucky I am. Three times before I turned forty, I should have been dead. But here I sit, friends around me, a girlfriend who is better than I deserve, and a business that keeps me on the waters of these Outer Banks. I shake my head with a smile, put the truck in gear and drive back home to the marina.

Chapter 17

I arrive at *First Draft* just after sunset and walk down the dock, lights atop power pedestals pointing down at the ground lighting my path. The Hatteras is dark as I scale the boarding stairs and step into the aft deck. From my left hand I drop my truck keys on the wet bar counter on the forward bulkhead and then open the salon door with my right. I step down the stairs ignoring the light switches on the wall at the top. I am not a fan of overhead lighting so I have placed a lamp at the bottom of the stairs that I can quickly turn on when I enter the boat. The air from the cooling system hits my skin, and I am thankful for the lower humidity and cool temperature. I turn on the lamp and look forward toward my desk. My chair is turned around and facing the door, a man in khakis is sitting in it. His left leg rests on his right knee revealing a brown, bare ankle just above a tan Topsider. His shirt is short-sleeved, white with buttons all the way down the front, a pocket on each breast has a button holding it closed. It's a Latin-looking garment which goes perfectly with his darker skin, brown eyes and black hair. He is clean shaven now, but I have seen his eyes before.

A few months ago while having lunch at *Duke's*, Scotty and I were talking with Junior about a body we had found floating in Albemarle Sound. We thought we were recovering the body of a teenage boy who disappeared while riding a Waverunner off the beach in Kitty Hawk. Instead, when Scott turned the body over, we were looking at a Hispanic guy with a bullet hole in his head.

Sitting at *Duke's* at a table near us were three Hispanic men, two laborers sitting across from another who was much more flashy. He wore pleated black jeans over shiny cowboy boots, a starched dress shirt and a bolo tie. They were just patrons in a restaurant at the time, but a picture shown to me by Magic as I recovered in the hospital changed all that.

The picture was of Miguel Cortez, the captain of the vessel that was being used for the human trafficking ring, and I recognized him immediately as one of the men sitting across the table from the flashy guy. The police were looking for information on the kingpin of the ring, an individual they knew only as *Jefe*. Realizing I had information for them, I shared what I could remember about him. While that man's face was hidden behind a neatly groomed beard at the time, his eyes are unmistakably the same as the man sitting in my salon.

"Hello mister Cooper," he says in accented English. "Close the door and have a seat," he says using the muzzle of the gun he is holding to point at the loveseat across the salon from him. I do as I am told.

"Do you know who I am?" he asks me, resting the pistol on his lap, the muzzle facing me, his hand still on the grip, a finger lingering above the trigger.

"I don't know your name, but I do know who you are and what you have done."

He smiles but it doesn't reach his eyes. "What I have done, Mr. Cooper?" he says, mocking me. "It's what you have done that brings me here."

"And what is that?" I ask before continuing. "You know my name, but I don't seem to know yours."

"My name is Oscar," he says proudly. "And what you have done is interfered with my organization. You have cost me a lot of money."

"Your organization is illegal Oscar," I say.

"I brought people to a better life," he begins before I interrupt.

"A better life?" I say not hiding my incredulity. I continue in a louder voice, "I personally saw two men who were killed by bullets from your… *organization*," I say, disgust dripping from the last word and leaning forward toward him.

He stops my progress by picking up his gun and pointing it at me. "And you can have a bullet of your own if you would like," he says, the muzzle just inches from my forehead.

"You are going to anyway, just do it now," I say, my words possessing more strength than I feel.

"No, Mr. Cooper," Oscar says. "Not here. Let's go for a ride, shall we?"

"If you are thinking about dinner, I already ate, but thank you," I say, fear channeling my inner wiseass.

Oscar laughs now. "You are a funny man, no?" he says. "I was thinking more about a drink," he continues pulling a bottle of Cuervo Tequila from a bag on the floor at his feet."

"I'm more of a Casamigos guy myself, but you feel free," I say.

"Shut up!" he says, all emotion leaving his face and leaning in closer behind his own gun. "You can joke all you want, Mr.

Cooper. That will all be over soon. Right now though, you need to go start the boat. We are leaving the dock."

"Aww, man, I wish I could…" I begin. The muzzle pressing against my forehead stops me.

"We go now," Oscar says, his head directing the way this time.

"Okay," I say. "We go." I stand and walk up the steps to the aft deck, and then turn left again and go up to the flybridge. Out of habit, I stop at the top and lean down to the starboard bulkhead and open the cabinet with the switch panel in it. I feel the gun in the back of my head and stop.

"I need to turn on the switches to start the engines," I say, holding my hands out where he can see them and hoping he doesn't question me any farther.

"Do it slowly," he says. I do as I am told turning on the switches for the electronics before standing and walking to the helm.

I remove the Sunbrella cover from the controls. I pull a switch that is on the face of the panel and the overhead light turns on. The gun is at the back of my head again. "Turn that off," Oscar says.

"But I need to see…"

"Off," he says quietly, emphasis delivered by the pressure of the muzzle behind my right ear.

"I wouldn't have picked you as a lights-off kinda guy, Oscar?" I say as I turn off the light.

He presses the muzzle harder into the skull bone behind my ear, the metal cutting the skin and drawing blood. "Just start the boat and let's go," he says.

My blood is dripping down my neck and into the collar of my ECU shirt. I do as I am told. I turn the port ignition key and mash the START button until the alarm sound stops. I do the same on the starboard side.

"Can I turn on the gauge lights?" I ask. I need to see that everything is running as it should. I will also need to turn running lights on or we will be stopped."

"Go ahead," he says.

I pull another switch and the gauges are revealed, the dim light just enough for me to read each of them. The navigation lights are on as well, but they are outside and not visible from our position. The diesel smoke travels on the south wind into the flybridge, the taste of diesel fumes filling my mouth.

"Will you go get the lines while I turn on the generator and unhook us from shore power?" I say to Oscar turning in the direction of the flybridge stairs, hoping to get down below and retrieve a certain weapon from the galley.

"No," he says, stopping me. "We will do it together. You go first." *Damn.*

I lead us down the stairs and back into the salon. As Oscar covers me with the gun, I turn the generator on, and then switch the power from shore to on-board. I head back up to the starboard side and unhook the shore power cord before dropping it to the dock. I have done this a hundred times and it is second nature for me.

With the wind pushing us away from the dock, I remove the two stern lines first before walking up to the bow. I undo the half hitch holding the starboard bow line and place it on the hook I installed on the pole. I repeat each of these steps with the port bow line. I then walk back to midship and remove the port side spring line, and then the starboard spring line and dropping each to the dock. We are now floating free. I check all navigation lights before stepping back to the helm, Oscar close to me the entire time. I step to the wheel and press the two buttons that activate the bow thruster joystick control. A quick tap to port on the thruster and we are in the center of the slip again.

I put both engines into forward for two seconds and when the vessel starts moving forward, I put them back into neutral allowing the wind and inertia to push us out of the slip. Looking aft I wait until the dive platform clears the pole on the port side before putting the port engine into forward, and then the starboard engine into reverse. First Draft spins perfectly on her center pointing her pulpit out toward the bay. Just before she evens up with the canal, I put the starboard engine into forward and we are on our way out of the marina.

"So, what is your plan, Oscar?" I ask as we idle out toward Shallowbag Bay. "Where are we off to?"

"Take us out to this location," he says, placing a piece of paper with map coordinates on it.

"I have to use my phone for GPS," I say.

"What about these?" he says pointing at the covered electronics on the helm.

"They don't work," I lie, hoping he doesn't ask me to remove the covers. "I don't go out much, so I use Navionics on my phone, or on the tablet that is sitting on my desk down below. If you want me to go here, then I need one or both of those."

At this point we are well away from the dock and he is comfortable enough to leave me at the helm as he goes below. He returns less than thirty seconds later holding my tablet in his hand. I lay the tablet onto the Nato mount magnet I have installed on the dash, and then press the button to turn it on. I tap the *Boating* icon and Navionics opens up showing a detailed map of the waterways all around us.

I press Route and then choose the *Automatic* option before choosing our current position as our start, and then the coordinates Oscar gave me as our destination. Navionics thinks for a moment and then places onto the map a path to take us there. I press START on the app and begin to follow the instructions. Our destination is more than five miles off Oregon Inlet. While not an unexpected development, I am not seeing much to be hopeful about at the moment.

We leave Shallowbag Bay and turn south under the Highway 64 bridge and into Roanoke Sound. The Bodie Island lighthouse blinks periodically to our east. "Go faster." Oscar demands.

While *First Draft* can go faster, she can't go much faster. I can certainly pick up our pace a little bit if I really want to. Our eight knots could be safely pushed to ten, but I am trying to prolong my evening as much as possible and going faster doesn't achieve that goal. You can call me selfish if you want. I'll take it selfish over dead any day. "We can push it a little harder, but we will likely overheat," I say. "I haven't cleaned the intakes in a long time." Technically, this isn't a lie. I, personally, have not cleaned them. Maria did.

"Do it," he says. Then he smiles a knowing smile. "I am aware of your bottom cleaning schedule."

What the hell does that mean? I wonder.

I press the throttles up just enough to get an extra knot out of them. Oscar begrudgingly accepts our slow progress and leans against the starboard helm seat, periodically looking at the tablet to determine our current location. We are more than fifteen nautical miles from our destination, almost two hours at this speed.

I think about Magic. She is probably finishing dinner right about now. I wonder how her evening went. I am hoping I get an opportunity to hear about it. Right now, the odds of that happening look poor.

Chapter 18

Magic is looking across the table at Sheriff Jefferies and the consultant as they talk to each other about her future. She is listening, but her mind keeps wandering. She turns in her chair and looks out the window of the 1587 Restaurant in Manteo, her black pepper seared tuna half-finished on her plate. Her gaze focuses across Shallowbag Bay to Ballast Point, the homes brightly lit by the sun beginning to set on the western horizon. There is a light chop on the bay as daily fishing charters are making their way back to the docks.

The consultant is a man named Carl. He is close to her own age, a good-looking guy with dark, wavy hair and a tan face that could have been pulled directly from an L. L. Bean catalog. Magic can picture him at the wheel of a sailboat, his hair blown back by the wind in his face. He has dressed casually for this meeting by replacing suit pants with khaki linen slacks, the legs pleated with cuffs at the bottom, his shiny loafers with sox alluding to a more formal outfit earlier in the day. He wears a blue button-down shirt, the starched collar creating a sharp edge in contrast to the dark suit coat. Light blue sleeves peek out the end of the jacket arms, his left wrist sporting a gold Rolex that costs as much as a small Japanese sedan. To complete the casual look, his shirt is open at the collar, his tie left behind on the passenger seat of his car. This is politics in the Outer Banks.

"What do you think, Magic?" Jefferies asks. Magic turns to look at the Sheriff, and then at Carl. She realizes she wasn't listening as well as she thought she was.

"Pardon me, say that again?" she asks, turning in her chair to give them her complete attention.

Carl answers for Jefferies, "We will do the announcement at the *First Friday* event in Manteo in November. The Sheriff will go first and announce his candidacy for the county judge position, and then he will introduce you as his successor. He will say a few words about you and why you are best to follow him as Sheriff, and then he will announce you. You will then thank the Sheriff, say some nice words about him and then talk about you and why you will be Dare County's next Sheriff."

"Will you write those words for me?" Magic says sarcastically.

Missing the tone, Carl answers, "If you would like me to."

"No, that's okay. I can handle it," Magic says, her annoyance no longer hidden.

Sheriff Jefferies can see that Magic is finished with this conversation. "Carl, thank you for all your help," he says. "We will talk more soon. Let me walk you to the door."

Carl looks around the table, and then, realizing the meeting is over, stands in his place. "Thank you Deputy Majik," he says.

"I look forward to working with you and seeing you sworn in as the next Sheriff of Dare County." He extends his hand toward her.

Magic stands and takes his hand, firmly shaking it. Annoyed or not, she knows her manners. "Thank you, Carl," is all she says.

"I'll be right back," the Sheriff says over his shoulder as he starts toward the front door, Carl one step in front of him.

Magic looks out the window again as darkness sets in over the bay. Her mind is wandering to Coop. She thinks back to the events that brought them together. The body Coop recovered in early summer reminded her of her brother who disappeared a decade ago. He was found months later, his body lifeless on a discarded mattress behind an ABC store in Raleigh. She was astonished when local Police didn't pursue the case. When she saw the same thing happening, she promised to find out the truth about what happened to the Hispanic man found floating on Albemarle Sound.

Stretched-thin police and Sheriff departments were fine with Magic and Coop pursuing the case on their own, and neither unit expected them to find anything. Instead, they discovered a second body in the pine brush along the shore of the Chowan River, and there was no longer any way to deny that something nefarious was happening in the Outer Banks of North Carolina.

Magic tried to remember how Coop first came on to her. Instead she recalled the way she had teased him, wearing bikinis she knew made the most of her athletic figure. Still looking out the window over the back of her chair, she remembers surfacing in the water near the boat and placing her top onto the dive platform of *Recovery*, looking up at Coop and inviting him to join her for a swim. She laughs at her boldness. No one would believe that it was her, and not him, who was the pursuer.

"What are you laughing about, Zaina?" she hears the Sheriff say behind her. She turns around and sees him smiling at her, clearly enjoying her moment of happiness. He also shows no remorse about interrupting it.

"Just thinking about the last few months," she says, shaking her head with a slight grin. "So much has happened."

"So, you were thinking about Coop, huh?" he says, reading her thoughts.

Magic laughs. "Yes, I was." *How does he do that?* she wonders.

"Well, I'm glad that man makes you smile." The Sheriff says, sitting back down at his place. The waiter comes to take the dirty plates and the Sheriff pushes his chair back slightly from the table. He looks up at the waiter and says, "Coffee please." The waiter nods as he is clearing the table and looks over at Magic.

"None for me, thanks," she says, before pushing her own chair away from the table and looking back out the window.

"Zaina," Jefferies says. "Look at me." His tone is fatherly, much as it has been for her entire life. He is more than a mentor to her. She turns and looks at him.

"Are you up for this?" he asks.

"Yes," she says strongly. "I am." She knows Jefferies doesn't like indecisiveness, so she makes the statement firmly. She isn't faking it; she has made the decision that she wants to be the next Sheriff of Dare County.

When these conversations started, this was not the case. She had no interest in running for political office, and honestly feared the politicking it would take to get elected. It didn't appeal to her at all. Working the human trafficking case with various departments in multiple jurisdictions changed that. She clearly became the point person of the effort, delegating tasks to each organization, even her own. She is a leader, and much of what she learned about leadership is because of this man across the table from her. She aspires to be the kind of boss Sheriff Jefferies has been to her, and while she may not like the politics part, it is a price she is willing to pay.

"Good," he says firmly as his coffee is delivered with the check. He hands the waiter his credit card before the portfolio is set down on the table. "We will have to discuss how your opponent will spin your relationship with Coop, you know that, don't you?"

"I do," she says. "And I don't care. He is more of a man than anyone they will put up against me." The Sheriff is loving her resolve and smiles as he takes a sip from a cup that looks very small in his hands. "He might even be a better cop too," she says, laughing now.

The Sheriff laughs and sprays coffee off the surface of the cup. Setting it down on the table and wiping his mouth with a napkin he says, "Please don't recruit him into the force." He is laughing loudly now.

"I won't, I promise," Magic says, laughing with him and leaning forward, touching his arm. "I think he is fine as a contractor, just the way you set it up."

"We are in agreement there," he says. His laughter settling, he looks a bit more serious and continues, "Let's find this guy, *Jefe*, Zaina. The work you have done to get to this point is stellar. Now we need to finish it."

"I'll get him," she says. "And I will find Angela too."

The Sheriff's face scrunches as he recalls their meeting from this morning. They decided that they will go to the hospital tomorrow and remove the machines from Miguel. "Do you want me to delay the removal of support?" he asks her.

"No. It's unfair to Miguel, and when we find Angela the stories of him being a noble man will be better than seeing him in the state he is in right now."

The Sheriff nods in agreement. "Then so it will be," he says, finishing his coffee as the check with his credit card is returned to him. Magic watches the Sheriff as he first pulls his credit card out of the portfolio and places it back in his wallet. She allows a small smile as she recalls how Coop never remembers to take his credit card. She normally does it for him, or they have to return to the restaurant to retrieve a forgotten one. The Sheriff adds a twenty percent tip, signs the merchant receipt and then copies the numbers down on the customer version, placing it in his wallet as well.

"Let's blow this popsicle stand," he says, pushing his chair back from the table and standing.

"No one says that," Magic says allowing a laugh.

"I say that, and that is all that matters," he says. "After you," he continues, sweeping his arm and hand in the direction of the front door.

Magic turns once more to the window. It is dark now. She sees the navigation lights of a lone vessel, the red port light disclosing that the vessel is heading away from the marina and out to sea.

Chapter 19

Outside the restaurant Magic gives Sheriff Jefferies a hug and a peck on the cheek. His car is parked directly in front of the restaurant, a black Dodge Charger with tinted windows and the word Sheriff stenciled in gold on the doors. He starts the engine. Magic can see his silhouette through the tint. He nods to her and roars out of the parking lot. He isn't going fast; a HEMI knows how to do nothing else *but* roar.

Magic reaches for her phone in her pocket before realizing she is wearing a dress. She inconspicuously checks her inner left thigh and feels some comfort in the small handgun that rests in a thigh holster there. This isn't her department Glock; this is a personal weapon she has for just this type of occasion, one requiring a dress instead of pants or shorts. It is smaller, but just as effective if the need arises. She unzips the small clutch in her hand and pulls out her phone, dialing Coop's number. It rings multiple times before she hears the message she has heard a thousand times. "We're sorry, the subscriber has not set up their voicemail."

She mashes the red button ending the call, then presses the green again. The result is the same. *Damn you Coop*, she thinks to herself. She was hoping to talk with him about the meetings. He should be waiting for her call, phone close by and ringer turned on. But she knows better than that. Coop isn't tied to his phone, and it's one of the things she loves about him. She decides to drive to the marina.

Magic walks to the parking lot at the end of Budleigh Street and steps up into her department Tahoe. She starts the engine, places the truck into drive and proceeds forward out of the spot she has backed into. She turns left onto Queen Elizabeth Avenue, and then right on Fernando street. Passing the Maritime Museum, she proceeds onto Agona Street for two blocks before turning south on

Highway 64. A few short minutes later, she turns left into the chute-like entrance for Shallowbag Bay Marina.

Normally at this time of night *First Draft* is lit up, the lamps from inside glowing and reflecting on the water, the blue LED lights on the aft deck a beacon leading directly to Coop's Hatteras. Instead, she sees nothing.

Magic accelerates to the parking spot behind Coop's slip, pulling out her phone at the same time. She hits the CALL button again. It defaults to the last number she called. This time it goes immediately to the automated message. "We're sorry, the subscriber…" Magic hangs up before it finishes. She begins typing a name into her phone, S, C, O. On the third letter Scott Parker's name is second in the list. She mashes his name and then the green button to make the call.

"Magic! How are…"

Magic interrupts him. "Scott, did Coop say he was taking *First Draft* out tonight?"

"Not to me, he didn't. Why, what's…"

Magic interrupts again. “I am at the marina and the boat is gone. Coop isn’t answering his phone.”

“I’ll be right there,” Scott says as he hangs up. Magic can hear him moving already.

Magic dials another number. “Deputy Majik, can I help you?” a confused voice says at the other end of the line.

“Yes, I need a trace on Coop’s mobile phone right now.”

While the request is delivered in a steady voice, he can hear the concern. Sheriff Jefferies doesn’t question why, he simply says, “I will make the calls and get back with you immediately,” before the line goes dead. Magic tries Coop’s phone one more time and it goes directly to the robotic voice again.

Magic sits at the wheel of her Tahoe not sure of her next steps. Scott is on his way and the Sheriff is getting a trace on Coop’s phone. Feeling helpless she slams the palm of her hand against her steering wheel three times and yells, “Dammit! Dammit! Dammit!” with each strike. Coop is forgetful and aloof much of the time, but she knows what kind of Captain he is. There is no way he leaves the dock without giving someone his float plan; where he is going, when he will arrive or when he will return. And there are only two people in the world he would give that information to; she is one and Scott is the other.

She sees the headlights of Scott's Chevy Silverado turn into the marina entrance. He is speeding and, even though she is an officer of the law, she is okay with him breaking the law right now. He pulls two spots beyond the Tahoe, screeching to a halt before the truck hits the curb. His driver door flies open and Scott Parker is on the pavement running to her driver side door.

Magic gets out to meet him and gives him a hug, holding him tight. "Coop's gone," she says to him trying to keep emotion out of her voice but failing.

Scott squeezes her tightly and asks, "What do you want to do?"

"He is on the water and that's where we need to be," she says, pulling away from him. She reaches into the open door of the Tahoe, uses her combination to open the center console and removes her Glock. Making sure it is loaded, she goes to put it into a belt holster before remembering she is wearing a dress. "Dammit!" she shouts again.

Magic opens the back door of the truck and grabs her holster belt. She slams both doors shut and says, "Let's go," walking down toward the Whaler. Scott pauses a second. *This is one badass woman*, he thinks to himself as he watches her walk away, dress fluttering in the breeze, holster in one hand and a pistol in the other. Magic is halfway down the dock before she realizes she is still wearing her heels. She kicks them off one at a time into the marina and steps barefoot onto *Recovery*.

Scott runs down the dock behind her and steps into the cockpit of the Whaler. Immediately he goes to the helm, lowers the Honda 225 four-strokes into the water and starts them up. Magic is already removing dock lines and in no time they are untethered and moving away from the slip. She is about to tell Scott to throttle up when her phone rings. It's the Sheriff.

"Talk to me," she answers the phone.

"His phone pinged out of the marina and heading south," the Sheriff says.

"Where is it now?" she asks.

There is a short pause on the other end. "The last ping we have is in the Pamlico near the mouth of the inlet." Magic knows he means Oregon Inlet.

"Go!" she tells Scott. Even though they haven't left the marina yet, he pushes the throttles to the stops and roars out into Shallowbag Bay.

"Where are we going?" he asks.

"Out the inlet!" Magic yells over the wind and engine noise.

They reach Ballast Point a few short minutes later and turn south under the Highway 64 bridge, running full speed into Roanoke Sound. Scott knows these waters, and knows this is not a safe speed, especially without the aid of instruments.

"Remove the covers from the electronics," Scott says, his voice loud enough to reach Magic over the cacophony. She does as he asks. He turns on the dashboard switch labeled, *ELECTRONICS*, and then presses the power button on each screen. Once they have finished their boot-up, he presses the *OK* button on each.

Scott and Magic look down at the radar looking for returns that might be coming from *First Draft*. Magic sees it first and grabs Scott's arm. He looks down at the screen and sees it too. A white triangle is on the screen just under fifteen miles away. They both look over to the GPS and see the same triangle but can now tell that its location is just inside of the inlet. They look back to the radar and check out the AIS information; this vessel is heading due east at nine point one knots. They also see that the vessel name is *Mary Elizabeth*.

"Damn!" Magic shouts in frustration. "I thought that was him!" She is punching the helm seat over and over in an effort to release her frustration.

It's Scott's turn to smile now. "Magic!" he shouts to her. "Stop!" he continues, grabbing her arm. "*Mary Elizabeth* was the name of *First Draft* when Coop bought her." He allows that to sink in for a moment. "It's him," he says.

Magic isn't sure how to show her elation. Instead she just says, "Go dammit! Go!"

Scott presses the throttles again, but they are already as far as they will go. He looks at the speed over ground on the GPS and does some quick math in his head. At thirty-eight knots they should reach the Hatteras in under an hour.

Chapter 20

I check the gauges as we progress toward the inlet. It's dark, but the moon's light is enough to keep my bearings. Oscar is quiet, looking periodically at the GPS display on the tablet, and then at his watch. It is a calm night, a coolness in the air but warm enough to keep the flybridge side isinglass open. I can smell the sand from the island beaches to our east. The diesels have settled into a rolling hum as small waves lap against the hull of the Hatters attempting to impede our progress. It would be a beautiful late summer evening cruise if the man next to me weren't holding a gun.

The song *Abracadabra* by Steve Miller is suddenly blasting out of the speakers on the helm. Oscar immediately reacts, stepping back and pointing the gun at me. "What is that?"

"It's the stereo," I say. "It turned itself on. It does that sometimes." I am lying again. I know full well that this is my ringtone for Magic. Abracadabra… Magic. Get it? My phone is below and connected to the Bluetooth receiver on the sound system. "It will stop," I say just as it does. "See?" I look over at Oscar, hoping he is buying it.

He settles for a moment but seems to be thinking about it. That's when the song starts again. He puts it together this time. He raises the gun to the side of my head and says, "Where is your phone?"

"What ph…" I don't get to finish the question. He rams the butt of the gun into the back of my head, not hard enough to knock me out, but enough for me to see stars and feel blood running down my neck.

"Charging on my nightstand in the master stateroom," I tell him. He runs down below to retrieve it.

I reach my right hand behind me and feel wetness in my hair, blood running from a gash at the bottom of my skull about an inch behind my right ear. I drag my fingers from the cut down to the scar in my neck and remember the feeling of my blood then. While the warmth and slickness are similar, there is nowhere near the amount that coated my hand that night. When it happened, I was at the helm of *Recovery* in pursuit of Oscar, although I didn't know him by name then. I bring my hand down from my neck and wipe it on my shirt leaving a streak across the front just below what's left of the letters, *ECU*. I return to steering the Hatteras, the drying blood sticky on the stainless steel.

Oscar comes back up to the helm holding my phone. He makes a show out of putting it up in front of my face, and then sending it flying through the starboard isinglass window out into the water. I am hoping I live long enough to replace it. It will probably the only time I take joy in buying a mobile phone.

"I hated that phone anyway," I say to him. He steps aggressively in my direction and I think he is going to strike me with the gun again. He stops just short of hitting me, but then leans his face in close to my ear.

"You will die tonight, Mr. Cooper," he says slowly, his warm breath moving the ends of dry hair the blood hasn't reached yet. "Speed up and get us to those coordinates." Then he yells in my ear, "Now!"

"You need a breath mint," I say.

Wham! The gun scrapes down the back of my head, the butt catching the collar of my shirt and ripping it before hitting a vertebra at the top of my spine. More warmth pours from my head.

"Okay," I acquiesce, raising my right hand toward him, palm out in surrender. "I have to navigate the inlet first," I say, turning east into Oregon Inlet. The sandbars in this area shift constantly, but this isn't my first rodeo. I can make it through, no problem. Still, I consider running the boat aground. I can get enough speed that the impact would throw Oscar off balance, perhaps giving me an opportunity to get the upper hand, even if just for a moment. Just as I am about to steer sharply to port, I change my mind. I continue out to the Atlantic Ocean, hoping that someone follows the electronic breadcrumbs I am leaving along the way.

"We're here," I say to Oscar thirty minutes later, pulling back on the throttles and checking the gauges. Everything looks good. Well, everything except for my future, that is.

"Shut the engines off," Oscar tells me. I do as I am told. "Turn off your lights." I follow his instructions again. We are dead in the water, floating free five miles off Pea Island, the wildlife refuge just to the south of Oregon Inlet. He raises his gun toward me and says, "Go downstairs."

"You mean, 'down below'," I correct him before he backhands me across the face, his ring cutting my cheek.

I decide that following his orders may be the better plan. First, I need to get him away from the helm. With lights no longer on and the instrument panel dark, there is a thin line of light escaping from one of the electronics' screens and I don't want Oscar to get curious. Second, he has suggested we go below and doing so will get me closer to my gun. *My gun.* As I think those words, I get uncomfortable with them, even in the circumstances I am in. I am a writer, or at least I was at one time. Until recently, my knowledge of guns was limited to writing copy against them for a gun control lobby. Now I wish I had one in my hand. Oh, how times change. I proceed down to the aft deck, and then down into the salon.

The moon is half full and low on the western horizon, its light giving the salon an eerie glow. Out of habit, I turn on the lamp at the bottom of the stairs. Oscars foot lands in the center of my back propelling me forward and making me lose my balance. I try to catch myself with my hands, but instead catch the corner of the galley counter with my face. My body spins around and I land hard, flat on my back with a thud, my head dangling over the top step that leads to the galley. *That's going to leave a mark*, I think as I look to the dark space between the refrigerator and the cabinet.

The light goes off and Oscar is standing above me pointing the gun at my chest. "Get up and sit in your chair," he says. I hold both hands in front of me, again surrendering to his request. I slowly stand, and then do as he said, turning and sitting in my desk chair.

Oscar sits in the loveseat across from me now. I think to myself that this is the opposite of how we were sitting earlier, not that it really matters. He pulls the bottle of tequila from the floor and opens the top. “Drink,” he says. I look at him, and then at the bottle.

“I can’t,” I say.

“Oh, I know all about your drinking problem Mr. Cooper,” he says. “It seems that tonight you have relapsed.” His smile is evil, and he holds the bottle up higher. He is proud of the plan he has come up with. “Drink,” he says, handing it to me.

“Let me get some glasses and ice,” I say and begin to stand.

“No,” Oscar says firmly, stopping me mid-stance. I sit back down. “From the bottle” he says.

There is enough light in the salon that I can see the dark liquid in the bottle and can even read the name Cuervo on the label. That probably comes more with years of experience than from my night vision.

"No one would ever believe I'd drink that shit," I tell him. "Where's the good stuff?" I am stalling, and he knows it.

"Now, Mr. Cooper," he says, in a hoarse whisper.

I reach out and take the bottle by the neck. I am practiced at this maneuver, and the familiarity is oddly calming. I bring the mouth of the bottle under my nose and sniff deeply, taking in the aroma. Immediately I feel the rush. I can feel its warmth in the back of my throat, holding my breath for a moment to savor the taste and the feeling. This is what I remember. Oh shit…

Other than the sound of an anxious wave lapping at the hull, the sea has been quiet around us. Now though, there is the unmistakable sound of outboard motors approaching, and by the high whine they are making, the boat is coming in hot. Oscar looks more curious than concerned as he looks down at his watch, stands to a squat and turns his head to the left so that he can see out the window facing west.

The motors are getting louder, and I recognize their hum. I have heard them hundreds of times. I allow myself a small smile. The calvary is coming. More specifically, *Recovery* is here.

Chapter 21

Recovery is flying over the waters of Pamlico Sound as Scott turns west to enter Oregon Inlet. He has run these waters since joining the Coast Guard twenty years ago, most of the time in bigger boats and at more speed. Still, he knows the dangers and pays close attention to the land, a shadow against the sea in the moonlight, and to the top of the line GPS on the helm. They have been running at full throttle since leaving Manteo, and Scott is thankful for the reliable Honda outboards and the seaworthy hull of the Boston Whaler Guardian.

Magic is looking at the Hatteras AIS information on the radar screen. Shortly after it entered the Atlantic Ocean it picked up speed to ten knots, but now the vessel speed is dropping. She waits a minute to see if there is any change, but there isn't. "They stopped, Scotty," Magic says over the noise. The radar is set at eight miles and she quickly calculates the distance. "Just over five miles," she says. "Go!"

"We'll get there," Scott says. "Eight minutes out. Call the Coast Guard and let them know where we are going!"

Magic had already called the Sheriff and has kept him aware of the Hatteras' progress. She picks up the microphone for one of the two VHFs.

"US Coast Guard, US Coast Guard, US Coast Guard," she begins. "Motor vessel *Recovery.*"

After a short pause, a tinny voice through the small speaker responds, "Motor vessel *Recovery*, United States Coast Guard, switch to channel seventeen, one seven."

"One seven," Magic says, and then turns the channel nob one notch to the right up to Channel 17. "US Coast Guard, this is *Recovery.*"

"*Recovery*, US Coast Guard," she hears.

"This is Sheriff's Deputy Zaina Majik," she says into the microphone. "We are approaching a vessel, Motor Yacht *First Draft*, five nautical miles due east of Pea Island, requesting assistance."

"Sit Rep?" the male voice says, requesting a situation report. Magic gives the dispatcher the AIS information and GPS coordinates. She then quickly tells the Coast Guard her story about arriving at the marina and noticing the Hatteras gone from the dock. She has to explain how she knows this isn't just an owner trying to get away from the world as is common across communities all up and down the east coast. It wouldn't be the first time it has happened. She is convinced that Coop has been kidnapped and is in danger, especially now that the vessel has stopped moving.

"We will be on-site in," Magic pauses as she looks at the screen and does some math. "Four minutes," she finishes her sentence.

"Dispatching cutter out of US Coast Guard Station Oregon Inlet, ETA to your location, fifteen minutes."

"Roger that, US Coast Guard," Magic says. "Standing by on one-six."

"One-six," she hears from the radio.

Magic presses the button on the face of the VHF returning the radio to channel sixteen, and then looks up through the windscreen. She is trying to locate *First Draft* on the horizon. She looks down at the GPS and radar screens and calculates that it should be directly in front of the Whaler. She looks up again, squinting her eyes and scanning left and right.

"There!" she says, pointing at a dark silhouette, a small dot that barely interrupts the horizon line. They are less than a mile away, just under two minutes. Scott looks where she is pointing and sees it. He adjusts his direction just slightly to starboard and is running directly toward it making no effort to mask their arrival.

Magic opens the console box in the helm seat and removes her Glock she stored there. She walks around the helm to the bow, checks her weapon, and then stands against the starboard gunwale. She and Scott had discussed this. He will run the Whaler directly to the Hatteras, delivering Magic on the swim platform. She will step aboard and tie off Recovery to the stern boarding ladder, before proceeding up onto the aft deck. Scott will then follow her.

Magic is still barefoot, her dress buffeted by the air passing past her as the boat makes its progress toward the Hatteras. *First Draft* is directly in front of her now and Scott begins to slow. Suddenly there is a loud BANG! and a flash of white light fills the windows in the salon. Then two more, BANG! BANG! in rapid succession, white bursts of light in the windows again.

Before Scott has the bow in the perfect position, Magic jumps onto the swim platform and runs up the ladder, forgetting the bow line. She crosses the aft deck, weapon up in front of her, flashlight under the barrel but not turned on. She reaches out and grabs the doorknob for the salon door, and quickly pulls it open, turning on the flashlight.

"Dare County Sheriff!" she shouts, scanning her light up and down, and then side to side across the salon. "Coop!" she yells as she runs gun-first down the stairs and into the salon.

Chapter 22

The bore of the bottle touches my mouth and I can feel a coating of tequila on my lips, a tingling sensation on my skin. A warm waft of alcohol-infused air fills my mouth. I am about to close my eyes and drink when I see Oscar look at his watch, raise to a squatting position and look out the window to investigate the incoming vessel. More importantly, I see the side of his face.

I am already gripping the neck of the bottle in my right hand, and in one quick motion I sweep my arm forward striking the side of his head with the bottom, the thick glass making a loud thud but not breaking. Oscar falls forward, his face hitting the windowsill on the way down. The momentum of my arm ends with the bottle above his head. I quickly bring it down with all the force I can muster. This time the bottle breaks into a handful of large pieces, the thud against his skull accompanied by the sound of shattering glass. The smell of tequila is instantly in the air as the liquid douses his head and runs across the floor. Oscar collapses face first onto the deck of the salon, blood pouring from a cut on the back of his head. *Take that, bitch!* I think to myself. *Now you know how it feels!*

He has fallen straight down and landed on top of his gun. I am about to move the table that separates us and try to take it from him when he starts to move. I am simply reacting now and I throw my side of the table up into the air so that it flips over and lands on top of Oscar. I spin quickly to my left and fall down the stairs from the salon to the galley, my head crashing into the refrigerator. The dim moonlight isn't enough to see details, but I find the space between the refrigerator and the cabinet by sliding my hand across the white door, a dark streak of my blood tracing my progress.

I can hear Oscar struggling to get up, the outboard motor outside very close now. I keep myself low so that I am behind the galley counter as I find the case under the Piggly Wiggly bag, and I quickly set it in front of me on the floor. I open the case and feel the gun and magazine just as I left them. I pick them up, pistol in my right hand, magazine in my left. I slam the magazine into the .45 and chamber a round with a loud *CLICK-CLACK.*

I hear the table fall to the floor and know that Oscar is getting up. I stand from behind the counter and see that he is already standing. In fact, he has his weapon pointing directly at me.

BAM! Oscar fires immediately. Instinctively I raise the HK and fire twice. *BAM, BAM!* Oscar is propelled back into the loveseat, the impact forcing him to sit down. His body is a shadow against the dark fabric, and I can't tell if he still has his gun or not. I step around the counter and slowly begin to come up the stairs into the salon, my gun in front of me pointed at Oscar.

I reach the top step in the salon when the aft door flies open and a flashlight is shined directly into my eyes, blinding me. I aim my gun up in the direction of the light when I hear a familiar voice say, "Dare County Sheriff!"

It's Magic. "Coop!" she yells and comes quickly down into the salon. She scans her flashlight quickly in the direction I was pointing when she burst through the door. She continues across the salon reaching me in two steps, turning her body as she goes, her flashlight finally coming to rest on Oscar. He doesn't look so good.

His white shirt has a red stain that begins in the center just above his sternum and runs all the way down the front. His eyes are open, his chin resting on his chest, head leaning so that his ear is almost touching his left shoulder. His right hand is resting in his lap, forearm on his thigh, palm-up, his weapon still in his grip.

"Dare County Sheriff, drop your weapon!" Magic shouts at him. There is no response. "Drop your weapon now!" she says more loudly. Again, no response.

Tentatively Magic steps forward in a shuffle, moving her left foot forward and then bringing her right foot up behind it, her Glock leading the way. As she gets close to Oscar she expertly kicks with her left foot, causing his gun to fall from his hand to the floor. She removes her left hand from the bottom of her pistol and feels for a pulse on Oscar's neck. After five seconds, she removes her hand and lowers her gun, shaking her head, *No*.

Magic turns to me and notices that I am still holding my HK up and pointed at Oscar. I might even be shaking a little bit.

"Coop," she says gently. "He's gone. You can lower your weapon now." She reaches out, placing her hand on top of my arms and applying a light downward pressure. I slowly lower my aim with her help. She reaches down to my hands and softly takes the gun from me. For a moment I am astonished at how she can go from Rambo to Bambi in a matter of seconds. I keep that thought to myself.

She reaches to the lamp that rests on my desk and turns it on. Seeing the VHF microphone on the bulkhead, she takes it in her hand and calls the Coast Guard.

After all the protocols necessary when speaking on a VHF radio, Magic says, "Threat neutralized, take your time guys."

"Would you like to expand on that Deputy?" the tinny voice at the other end says.

"Not over open channels," Magic answers. "All souls accounted for," she says truthfully. One may not be alive, but he is accounted for.

"Roger that," the Coast Guard answers. "On our way."

Oscar is obviously dead. I have seen a few dead bodies, and he qualifies. I am shaking. It was him or me, I know that. He shot, I reacted. I just had better aim, that is the difference tonight. I shiver. Still, I just killed a human being. There is a hole in the center of his shirt, and one more in the wall above his head. Water is dripping down from it, probably the water line for the aft deck sink.

Magic looks and sees it too. "Double-tap?" she asks, pointing her thumb at the wall and turning to face me with a wry grin.

Despite everything else, I laugh. I am thankful for the release. "Maybe," I say, with a smile.

Chapter 23

We hear *Recovery*'s outboards idling up to the Hatteras. "Scott's here," Magic says. "I saw the gunshots and forgot to grab the line for *Recovery* when I jumped on." Carrying her Glock Magic walks out to the aft deck. I follow her up and out admiring her back side as she goes. She sticks her head over the stern rail and says, "All good…" stopping her words and her progress in mid-sentence.

"Hello," I hear a woman say, her accented voice immediately familiar. "You look surprised," she says. Magic's left hand is at her side just behind her thigh. She holds her hand wide open so I can see it, instructing me to stay where I am, and to be quiet. I do as I am told.

"Throw your gun into the water," Maria tells Magic.

"Take it easy," Magic says. "I'll do as you say. Don't hurt him." I realize she is trying to tell me that Maria has Scott, but also that he is alive and unhurt. Magic slowly turns her gun over so that it is suspended upside down between two of her fingers, her left hand up in surrender. She extends her arm and drops the Glock into the ocean. I slide across the floor closer to the aft rail, trying to get a glimpse of what is happening off the stern of the boat.

"Where is Oscar?" Maria says. "I'll take him, and we'll go."

"He is below, unable to come up here at the moment." It's not a lie, but it is certainly meant to mislead Maria into thinking he is still alive.

"Get him!"

"He killed Coop," she says, emotion in her voice. "I can't let him go." Okay, that is a lie. She delivers it skillfully though, and I would believe if I wasn't me. I am most definitely not dead. I slide a little farther and can now see through the chock on the starboard stern corner of the deck. Maria is holding Scott around the neck with one arm, her own pistol to his head. She is looking up at Magic.

I look at Scott's face, and while it is dark, there is enough moonlight to see the discouraged look on his face. It's not fear. It's more being pissed at himself for being duped. His eyes are squinted, and he is gritting his teeth, thinking that this woman got close to us, and now I'm dead. I want to tell him that we were both duped by Maria, he shouldn't be so hard on himself. I also want to tell him that I am most definitely not dead. I try to make eye contact with him through the chock, but he doesn't see me.

"Shoot her, Magic," he says through gritted teeth.

"Shut up," Maria says, but she does it quietly and tightens her arm around his throat. Scott's head leans back as his chin is lifted with the force.

"I'll get him," Magic says doing as she was asked, turning to walk back inside.

"Stop!" Maria yells this time, realizing the flaw in her instructions. She takes the gun off Scott and points it up at Magic. She looks flustered for the first time, like she doesn't know what to do. She points the gun back at Scott.

Magic returns to telling the truth and says, "The Coast Guard is on its way. You can still get out of here. Leave Scott, take the boat and go. I am keeping Oscar." She says his name for the first time and I can hear the disgust in her voice. Maria is looking at Magic, and then to Scott, quick glances in each direction. She is contemplating Magic's offer. I slide farther across the floor trying to get a little closer. My foot hits one of the chairs I have on the aft deck. The rubber footer chafed through long ago and the sound of it scraping across the floor is loud.

Maria turns in my direction with her eyes and the gun, and fires through the thin screen that extends from the top rail to the floor of the deck. Fiberglas dust fills the air above my head and showers down on me, her bullet hitting the ships bell with a loud, *CLANG*!

I am sure that Magic moves quickly, but I am seeing it all in slow motion. She reaches across her body and lifts the front of her dress. I wonder where this is going until I see her remove a small pistol from what looks like beige Spanx wrapped around her upper thigh. In quick succession she raises the pistol, levels it in Maria's direction and fires once. I look through the chock and see Maria's left shoulder explode with blood, her body twisting away from Scott, her gun falling from her hand as she loses her balance and falls over the gunwale into the water. Magic is down the ladder onto the dive platform before I can even get up.

A moment later I hear a splash and when I stand up and look over the rail, Scott is no longer in the Whaler. He is in the water, swimming to Maria who is flailing trying to keep herself afloat with one arm, the other incapacitated by the bullet lodged in it. Scott takes one of her arms by the wrist, first pushing her away from him, but then twisting her wrist turning her onto her back and pulling her to him in one quick motion. He puts the other hand in her left armpit and lifts, keeping her above water. Maria winces in pain, but Scott doesn't stop. Holding her this way, he scissor-kicks back to the Hatteras, and then deftly hands her up to the platform with one arm. Magic pulls her farther up where she begins to administer first aid applying pressure directly to Maria's wound. Scott lifts himself out of the water and onto the deck in one swift motion.

"Coop! Get the first aid kit!" Magic yells up to me. I run up to the flybridge, find the kit beneath the port bench seat and run back to the aft rail. There isn't enough room on the dive platform, so I hand the kit down and stay on the aft deck. I wouldn't be any help down there anyway.

I see red lights in the distance before I hear the engines. Two Coast Guard cutters are approaching swiftly, their route directly in the path of light created by the half-moon on the west horizon.

I look back down at the platform. Magic has a large gauze pad pressed tightly against Maria's s shoulder; Scott is holding her wrist with one hand while looking at his watch on the other, checking her pulse. These two are professionals. After everything this woman has done, here they are fighting to save her life.

"Don't let me die," Maria says weakly. "I have information for you," she continues, looking up at Magic.

"What information could you possibly have that I would care about?" Magic replies, her voice showing the disdain she has for this woman. Yet, she continues administering life-saving aid.

"The little girl," Maria says, "Angela."

I can see Magic tense up at the mention the girl's name. Until this point, Magic has been working from the top of Maria's head; they are looking at each other upside down. Magic shifts her body so that she is facing Maria in the same direction, never taking pressure off the wound.

"What do you know about Angela?" she asks calmly. The Coast Guard cutters are less than half a mile away and closing quickly.

Maria looks like she is going to fall asleep. Magic shakes her by pressing down on the wound again and again. Maria's eyes open wide. "What about Angela, Maria?" Magic says loudly directly into Maria's face.

The cutters are here, the first pulls its port rail broadside to our stern, the other floating just off its starboard side. One of the Coasties steps off the cutter and joins the party at the stern. "We'll take her from here," he says, kneeling at Maria's head where Magic was a moment ago. Scott gets out of the way by doing a pull-up lifting his body weight up and over the aft rail and landing on the deck. This is a maneuver I could never achieve, and I want to tell him that, but there are more important things right now.

Another Coastie steps to where Scott was and lifts Maria's feet as the other puts his hands under her shoulders. "Wait!" Magic says as they lift Maria, suspending her above the dive platform.

"What about Angela?" Magic asks one more time, her voice as loud as I have ever heard it.

The Coasties place Maria on the gunwale, two more Guardsmen attending to her from the cutter.

Maria looks up at Magic. Her eyes are wandering as the men work to secure the bandage on her shoulder. The pain of compression seems to wake her for a moment. She stares directly into Magic's eyes.

Just before passing out, Maria says, "I know where she is."

Scott, Magic and I are sitting in chairs on the aft deck. The Coast Guard cutter is rafted off the starboard side of *First Draft*. They retrieved Maria's boat and it is tied to the outside of the cutter. *Recovery* is secured on the port hip. The Coasties have gone below to assess the situation and asked us to sit tight as they do. We are drifting closer to shore but are still more than four miles off the coast. The moon has set and the stars in the sky are incredible. I am sitting next to Magic, holding her hand.

"Did I tell you that you look pretty tonight," I say to her, squeezing her hand.

"Thank you," she says with a roll of her eyes, squeezing my hand and pulling my arm toward her. She lays her head on my shoulder for just a moment before quickly sitting up in her chair and looking over at me. She runs her hand over my right shoulder feeling the fabric of my shirt crusted with blood.

"You look like shit," she says, laughing. She is right, I do. When I inspected myself earlier in the mirror of my stateroom, I saw the blood covering my right ear, red streaks covering my right arm. I have a fat lip and the beginnings of a black eye. The front of my shirt has streaks of blood that show black against the purple fabric. I can feel each of the wounds now as I sit with her.

"I'm getting too old for this shit," I say, and smile at her. She doesn't get the *Lethal Weapon* reference and I again vow to tutor her on this soon.

Our laughter subsides and the events of the night begin to settle in. I think about where we are right now; how we got to this point, and all that has happened. I killed a man tonight. He deserved killing, but that isn't in my job description. I run a boat and remove detritus from our waters. I try to convince myself that this is the same thing.

My hands begin to shake involuntarily, and I squeeze Magic's hand a bit harder trying to stop them. She reaches across with her other hand and wraps it over the top of mine, holding them still. "I know, Coop," she says, looking into my eyes. "I know." She runs her hand down my shirt, pausing it at my heart and pressing for a moment before sliding it down the bloody shirt front. She is looking at her hand as she takes the fabric in her fingers and rubs it together like she is cleaning glasses with it. She looks up at me lovingly and says, "Can I ask you something?"

I lean in closer to her face and say, "You can ask me anything."

Magic smiles, looks away a moment as though she is bashful. She looks directly into my eyes, pulls the shirt in her hand, as though wanting me closer, and asks, "Now can we throw this shirt away?"

Chapter 24

I wake up in Magic's bed. She is resting next to me, her nakedness so close I can feel the heat of her body even though we are not touching. The thin top sheet is all that covers us, its drape following her every curve, my eyes scanning from top to bottom. At the same time, I use my hands to investigate the injuries I incurred during last night's activities. I have two deep cuts in my head, one behind my right ear, the other on the back of my skull. A crusty mass of hair runs across each, the tangle done purposely by the Coast Guard paramedic as he used my own hair to close the wounds.

I move my fingers to my face. My bottom lip is fat and I feel a sting when I find a small cut where the thin skin of the lip meets the thicker skin and stubble below it. The lump under my left eye is pronounced, protruding almost an inch off my face. I examine my cheeks and neck and can feel puffiness everywhere. I attempt facial gestures but the swelling is restricting the muscles, each movement sluggish and painful.

I don't normally stay at Magic's, but my home is not in my possession at the moment. The Coast Guard took control of *First Draft* sealing it off as a crime scene and then towing it in so that local LEOs can do their investigation. I always wanted to say, *local LEOs* when talking about local law enforcement officers. I promise to not do it again.

After the Coasties hooked up the Hatteras and began slowly towing her in, Scott, Magic and I jumped into *Recovery* to run back to the marina. Scott stood at the wheel while Magic and I sat in the helm seat and held each other. "She's alive, Coop," Magic said to me quietly. "Angela is alive." The tautness in her body that is normally associated with conversations about Miguel's daughter is gone. She squeezes me tighter as she says this, and I can feel a renewed energy in her embrace. Still, this release is accompanied by tears. Magic is crying too. We arrived back at the dock just before daylight.

Now in bed, Magic's back is facing me, and I again pause a moment more to admire her shape through the sheet. I turn on my side and reach out, tracing her curves starting under her right arm, stopping my progress when my hand rests on her hip. I hear a low moan coming from somewhere deep inside her body, and I take that as an invitation to move closer. I slide across the center of the bed over to her side. The warmth of her body increases as I close the gap between us, but it is much hotter when we finally touch.

Magic rotates her body back into me, eliminating any space that was left between us. She turns her head up and around, a tired smile on her face. I lean in and kiss her, lingering on her mouth and pulling her closer.

"What time is it?" she asks.

I look over at the clock on her side table, and read it as I kiss her neck, my hands beginning to explore her body some more.

"Nine-thirty," I say. I can feel her moving out of the bed before she says a word.

"Crap!" she says running toward the shower. "We have to go!"

Then I remember. "Crap!" I say, jumping out of bed and following her toward the shower. She stops me with a hand to the chest.

"We will never get there if you get in this shower with me," she correctly states. "Guest shower, now!" she says pointing over my shoulder.

In moments we are both showered and dressed, and sexually frustrated. I'm pretty sure where we are going will dampen our spirits and eliminate any desire we are currently feeling. Magic grabs her keys and a minute later we are out the door and on our way to the hospital. In less than an hour we are removing Captain Miguel Cortez from life support.

Magic and I walk into Miguel's room. The Sheriff is already there, standing over Miguel saying a silent prayer. The man always amazes me. He is big, he is smart, he is religious, and he does what he says he will do. I wish all politicians were more like him. I look at Magic and know she will be a great Sheriff too.

Dr. Spencer Washington is walking around Miguel checking monitors and making notes on pages secured to the clipboard he is carrying. His small stature and rapid movements are in stark contrast to that of the statue-still, hulk of the Sheriff. Spence moves so quickly his lab coat flows behind him like a wedding train. The Sheriff's tan suit is pressed and hangs perfectly from his six-foot-six frame.

Jefferies turns toward us. He is wearing a red tie, his tan suit coat adorned with an American Flag pin on his left lapel. He walks over to Magic and gives her a fatherly hug. He releases her and puts his hand out to shake mine.

"You look like shit, Coop," he says deadpan.

"And you look, *Mah-velous*," I say in my best Billy Crystal. The Sheriff laughs as he shakes my hand and pulls me in for a pat-on-the-back man hug. When we release Magic is looking at us, the expression on her face saying, *What the hell was that?* I have so much to teach her.

The Sheriff reaches out and puts a huge paw on my shoulder. "You okay today?" he asks.

"I am," I say with a bit more confidence than I feel. *Fake it 'till you make it*, they say.

"Bullshit," he says, "but you will be, I promise you." His hand squeezes on my shoulder and I am happy he is on my side. I give him an appreciative smile and he releases me from his grasp.

A man who is obviously an attorney walks into the room. He is carrying a stack of papers and sets them down on the table under the window across the room. I can see that there are a significant number of pages that have colored tabs sticking out with the word, *SIGN* in capital letters on them. He organizes the pages and then turns to face us.

"Sheriff, it's time," he says lifting a pen for him to take. Jefferies takes the pen and steps up to the paperwork.

"Zaina, do you want me to wait longer?" he asks Magic.

"No sir," she answers. "This is unfair to Miguel, and when we bring Angela home, her last memories of him won't be this." The Sheriff nods and turns back to the table. The attorney begins turning pages for him explaining each before Jefferies scribbles his name on the appropriate line.

Magic and I step over to Miguel, Magic lifting his hand in hers. "I'm going to find her, Captain," she says, a tear escaping her right eye and running down her face. I look at her and admire again how beautiful her strength is. I recognize the look in her eyes and know that the tear is both sadness and contentment. Miguel's last conversation on this Earth was with Magic asking her to find his daughter, and she promised him that she would. Now, holding his hand and looking into his motionless face, she knows that she will be able to keep that promise. "Lo prometo," she reaffirms.

The Sheriff completes the paperwork and joins us at Miguel's bedside. He takes the man's other hand and looks down at him. "Thank you, Mr. Cortez," he says. "May your daughter know the strength you have, and how much you love her." I am moved, and I feel like I should say something. In a rare moment of thinking before I speak, I decide that I have nothing more to add to these sentiments. The Sheriff nods to Dr. Washington.

Standing outside the room a nurse notices we are ready and walks in to assist Spencer. Silently but efficiently they walk around Miguel, and around us. We are on either side of the bed, Magic and Jefferies holding one of Miguel's hands. I am standing behind Magic. I notice how easily Spence and the nurse avoid running in to us and realize this is not their first time. I can't imagine what it must be like to have to remove life support even once, much less to have done it so many times that you can accomplish the grisly chore without disrupting family members in attendance. We are not related, but we are Miguel's family today.

As each machine is shut off it gets quieter in the room. Ambient sounds carry in from the hallway now, and Spence and the nurse finish their work. We stand quietly and wait for the Doctor to tell us when he is gone.

Spencer takes his stethoscope and puts the round end to Miguel's chest. He stays in that position for more than five seconds before moving it under the left armpit. He does the same on the right side. Dr. Spencer then reaches up and removes the intubation tube that is down Miguel's throat, and then repeats the stethoscope checks. He steps away from the bed and makes a note on the clipboard. We are waiting for the time of death.

Dr. Washington begins to walk out of the room when the Sheriff speaks up. "Time of death?" he asks.

"There is no time of death, his heart is beating, and he is breathing on his own," is the answer we get. Magic looks down at Miguel and then up at me. Her face is beaming with hope. If I haven't said it before, I love the look of hope in Magic's eyes. It gives me hope too. I smile back.

"What should we do?" the Sheriff asks before the doctor can leave.

"We will monitor him and make assessments and a prognosis over the next few hours," Dr. Washington answers. His

Asperger's is on full display, his eyes avoiding direct contact like they are the positive side of a magnet to our negatively charged ones.

Magic looks at the Sheriff and asks, "Do you know where Maria is right now?"

"As of this morning she was out of surgery and in a recovery bed in the trauma unit," he says.

Magic grabs my hand and pulls, leading the way out of Miguel's room and down the hallway to the elevator. She pushes the *Down* button and we begin to wait patiently. Magic is edgy and she grabs my hand again, running to the end of the hall and shoving open the door labeled, *Stairs*. She is moving quickly in her low heels, and I am trying not to trip and take us both out.

We reach the bottom floor and she bursts through the door into a busy hallway, a gurney that was about to roll by stops abruptly, the intern at the top getting the handle in his gut.

"Sorry!" Magic says as she continues down the hall and through a door marked *Recovery*. As I look at the label, it is the first time I make the connection to my own boat's name. I remind myself that my disorder is a medical condition too.

Magic races up to the circular desk in the middle of the Trauma lobby and asks one of the women behind the desk where she can find Maria. She shows her badge as she does this. It's kind of hot.

The woman points us in the right direction and we quickly make our way to the door and enter her room. Maria is laying in the bed, her shoulder bandaged up and there is an IV bag on a pole, its tubing running to her left hand. Other than that, she has no devices, mechanical or otherwise, attached to her. She will live.

Maria looks tired, but she is awake. Her attention moves from the window to our entry, and then to Magic as she comes to Maria's side. "Angela Cortez," she says to Maria. "Where is she?"

Maria looks at me, and then out the window before she faces Magic again. There is feeling in her eyes and I almost feel sorry for her.

"I didn't know who she was, I swear," Maria starts, her accent stronger now than it was when we first met.

"I don't care Maria," Magic says. "You've done some terrible things. Do the right thing now," she continues taking Maria's hand. "Please."

Maria looks like she is about to cry, and then she does. Tears are streaming out of her eyes down the side of her face and onto the pillow beneath her head. She can't look at Magic.

Magic gently touches the side of Maria's face, wiping away a tear and turning her head so that they are facing each other again. "Please," Magic says softly.

Maria raises her right arm and wraps her hand around Magic's wrist, squeezing it gently as she returns her gaze, tears still running down her face.

Maria looks directly into Magic's eyes and says, "New Bern."

THE END

Acknowledgements

As I finish the final re-write of *REVENGE*, the world is in a very strange place. I am personal distancing by living on my boat in Beaufort, North Carolina, the COVID-19 Pandemic requiring great change in many of our lives. I have been here for almost a month working "from home" on my full-time job as well as finishing this work.

Diversions from the real world have come in multiple forms for me. I have been reading my favorite authors, two books by Ed Robinson and one by Rodney Riesel. I have tried each evening to take a boat ride on my Boston Whaler, the temperatures finally getting warmer in eastern North Carolina. I have also been escaping into the fictional world of Coop and Magic.

Whatever you are doing right now, if you are reading this, I want to thank you for giving my story some of your precious time. Whether you are reading while distancing during the pandemic, or you picked it up years later, I hope it delivers some escape for you as well.

Thank you to my early readers, John Cooper, Michael Doolittle, Annette Waisner and Captain Matthew ("Hoop") Hooper. Each makes my work better in a different way, and all make me a better writer. I read carefully the corrections and recommendations and am humbled by how much love I witness during our chats about these characters.

A special "thank you" to Cyber Warfare Operator for the US Airforce Alex Scalf whose weapons expertise contributed greatly to the scene where Magic is teaching Coop how to shoot. My goal was to not sound like the gun novice that I am, and if I still do, that is completely my fault. Don't let "Cyber" fool you; he knows his stuff.

To my daughters who are always in my mind as I write the character of Zaina Majik; you contribute to her strength, her confidence and her quick-witted sarcastic humor. I am proud every day of the women you have become.

And to Sarah, who puts up with me as I commit chunks of our time to this fictional world. Your support is invaluable, especially as I read aloud chapters for your review when you would prefer to go to sleep. Your critical ear improves my writing, and your love improves me.

I take liberties with locations and timelines, but I do strive to keep them as real as possible. Any mistakes or inconsistencies that remain are solely mine.

To all… Thank you.

Doug Brisotti
April 2020
Beaufort, North Carolina

About the Author

Photo Credit: Ella Brisotti

Doug Brisotti splits his time living on land in Greensboro North Carolina and on a boat in Beaufort (NC). He grew up on the water on Long Island, first in Glen Cove and then in Bay Shore, spending family vacations on Peconic Bay in Mattituck. After Guilford College and ten more years in North Carolina, Doug spent fifteen years in south Florida before moving back to Greensboro to be close to his daughters.

Doug is a licensed Captain and runs charters out of Beaufort (www.NextChapterCharters.com). More likely he can be found in his 17' Boston Whaler Montauk, *storyteller,* hanging out on a sandbar or having a drink with friends at a local watering hole.

Doug works for Curtis Media Group in Raleigh. He has two college-aged daughters, Kira and Ella, and lives with his "crew," his love Sarah and their ani-mates Lyla (dog) and Nahla (cat).

Previous Work

Non-Fiction

I'm Okay

2017

Fiction

Recovery; a Grayson Cooper Adventure

Outer Banks Series, Episode 1

2019